C000099867

SEDUCED BY A PRINCE

TANYA ANNE CROSBY

OLIVER HEBER BOOKS

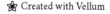 Created with Vellum

For the first time in his life, Merrick was speechless at the sight of a woman.

If he wasn't dead, surely he must be dreaming.

And then his angel shouted in his ear, and he knew he wasn't dreaming. She was a flesh-and-blood woman, and he wanted suddenly to kiss her... until her words penetrated.

"It serves the wretch right!" she declared, her breasts rising with indignation. "He's not hurt! He's just too muddled to ride! Rotten cad!"

"Nay, Miss Chloe! The horse threw him—I swear it! We saw it with our own two eyes!"

"Who the devil is 'we'?" she questioned.

Bloody shrew; she must be his wife.

"Och!" she snapped before Merrick could ask who she was. "He's bleeding all over my dress!" And she promptly dropped him to the ground.

And then he did what no manly man should ever do —he passed out.

THE PRINCIPALITY OF MERIDIAN,
1803

*H*ow can you believe he would marry you?

He was a prince, after all, she only an impoverished earl's daughter. Julian Merrick Welbourne III would command a nation someday, while Fiona no longer even had a home left to return to.

Indulging in a rare moment of self-pity, Lady Fiona Elizabeth MacEwen sat on the immense claw-footed bed that dominated her guest room. The fine, silk cloth rumpled beneath her bottom. This room, where she'd been confined since the birth of her twins, was no more than a luxurious cell. No doubt, she felt more like a prisoner than a guest.

Outside, there were no trees to shade the room from the heat of the day; the afternoon sun, diffused through gold-chiffon draperies, burnished the entire room with a gilded light that made one feel as though one simmered in the belly of a furnace. It was devilishly hot in this country—so unlike her beloved Scotland.

What a despicable mess she'd made of her life.

Fiona fought her tears. Her father hadn't raised a wilting violet. Nor had he raised an imbecile. She understood perfectly well why Julian was marrying that *other* woman. As the only son of Meridian's sovereign, he was expected to marry for the good of his country, not for love. She simply couldn't comprehend how he had forgotten his obligations to begin with—though perhaps he hadn't? Perhaps she'd never been more to him than a final rebellion?

That revelation made her feel used, abused and deceived.

Her eyes stung bitterly. Had he truly never loved her? Had he brought her to this palace only to become his mistress?

Alas, she would rather die than be any man's Jezebel!

A single tear slipped down her cheek. The worst of it all was not that she would never be wed to the man she thought she loved... but that she would never be wed at all.

What man would marry her with two little bairns in tow?

And worse, because of her damnable pride, Glen Abbey Manor—their ancestral home—was no longer her sanctuary. Even if Julian released her, she had nowhere to go.

Her heart squeezed painfully at the thought of her father—a mere guest in his own home.

They'd had so little to offer as a dowry and they'd both been so deliriously joyful over Fiona's good fortune at marrying so well, that her papa had sacrificed everything to see her dream come true. Trusting in the word of a gentleman, long before the impending nuptials, her father handed over the deed to Glen Abbey Manor. For four hundred and twenty-two years her kinsmen had been proud to call that manor their home. From Chreagach Mhor to the woodlands that spilled into McClellan's valley, all of Glen Abbey was a part of their legacy. The little church in the grove was even rumored to have sheltered the Stone of Scone when Edward of England sought to steal it for his own.

If her father was left wanting, it wasn't in honor or in charity. He'd shared his legacy quite generously, allowing the townsfolk, who'd settled the land along with their ancestors, to occupy their parcels without payment.

What would become of those people now?

How foolish they had been—how very, very foolish. And the greatest irony of it all was that Julian hadn't even wanted or needed Glen Abbey. Bordered by the Alps and the Mediterranean Sea, the Principality of Meridian covered no more than two square miles, but it was one of the most valuable pieces of real estate in all of Europe.

In comparison, the only value Glen Abbey held was as a means of control. She had no doubt Julian would use it now to control her life and that of her sons.

Shortly after the church bells struck two, a sharp rap sounded at the bedroom door.

Fiona didn't stir herself from the bed; her time to avoid this moment was long past. At any rate, she knew it would be him. The maid had a key and never bothered to knock.

Julian also had a key; he turned it in the lock to allow himself in. She heard the lock click, the door creak on old iron hinges, and then, dark and beautiful, he stood in the doorway. Her breath caught at the sight of him—as it always did. But she loathed this weakness within herself—that she could love this man, despite that he'd treated her so shabbily.

For only an instant he glanced downward, as though ashamed, and then said, "I've come to see my sons."

"I want to go home," Fiona countered, though she knew it would gain her naught.

3

Julian's handsome face was stern, his chiseled jaw clenched with iron resolve. His blue eyes were as pale as a new moon, silvered with lack of emotion. "As I have already explained, Fiona, I cannot allow you to leave with my children."

He stood gazing at her, his presence large, and she noted little sway in his posture. He would never let her go—not with her sons.

Fiona couldn't help herself; a tear escaped, sliding down her cheek. She ignored it. So did he as he crossed the room, toward the crib.

"I really don't believe you ever loved me," she accused him, swallowing her pride, feeling defeated. "If ever you did, you wouldn't keep me here to suffer the sight of your bride."

He said nothing and she took some comfort in anger. "Tell me, Julian, will it please you to know I will be sitting here cradling our bairns as your wedding bells toll?"

He walked past her, toward the window, without looking at her and she added, "I wonder how pleased your Elena will be when she learns of my presence in her home." To her dismay, she started to cry.

Julian stopped, at last, and turned to face her, his gaze softening. "Please... don't cry," he said, and for an instant, when he met her gaze, she saw a glimpse of the man she thought she'd known. It squeezed at her heart.

Unbidden, he came and sat beside her upon the bed, reaching out to swipe the tear from her cheek with a steady finger. Fiona closed her eyes, wincing over the tenderness in his touch.

"Fiona," he pleaded, "I could make you happy, if only you'd allow it. I would shower you and my sons with gifts. I would take good care of you. I would never disappoint you."

4

"You already have," she said, eyes swimming as she looked at him.

"Only think on it," he begged.

Fiona shook her head adamantly. "I will *never* be your mistress, Julian," she said with more conviction than she felt.

He reached out to touch her hand, and she moved it away. "You know how I feel about you," he said, but his confession professed nothing. He hadn't said those three words to her since the day he'd revealed his plan to wed another woman. If he dared to say them... if she heard them... her will to resist would have crumpled. But he hadn't said those three little words.

"My darling," he beseeched. "I promise to give you my full devotion."

Fiona's brows collided, and she said with acid sweetness, "You mean, when you aren't otherwise devoted to your wife and *her* children?"

He looked away guiltily. "Fiona," he begged. "You know it was not my choice to wed Elena."

Fiona didn't care to hear it. She swallowed her tears, summoning the last of her strength, and stood, turning her back to him. "All I know is that I will not disgrace my father's name any more than I have. As it is, I may never be able to face him again."

She walked away, needing distance, lest she be tempted. She still couldn't look at him without longing to leap into his arms to beg him to love her and her children.

How pitiful she felt.

Across the room, waking in their crib, the babes began to whimper, and Fiona rushed over to the cradle, grateful for the distraction. She touched each of their little cheeks, caressing them with a finger, their sweet little noses.

Merrick and Ian were everything to her. For them

5

she would bear any shame, endure any trial. At the very least, if he must lock her away from the world, he'd been merciful enough to leave her with her precious darlings.

"Mother adores you," she cooed. Already they looked so much like their father, with dark hair and eyes so deep a grey they were like storm-ridden skies.

Merrick seemed the more content of the two and she scooped Ian into her arms, intending to soothe him first.

She hadn't heard Julian approach, but his voice broke when he spoke, startling her. "I had hoped it wouldn't come to this, but you are, indeed, correct, Fiona." He put a hand upon her shoulder and squeezed very gently. "I cannot keep you against your will."

Fiona choked back a sob, anticipating what he was about to do. She wanted to go home—she did—but it pained her so much to leave him... never to see him again... never to have the chance to hold him.

"As you know, Elena will be arriving soon. I'll not have her unsettled by my mistake."

Mistake?

Fiona's throat constricted. If Julian had wished to hurt her, he couldn't have chosen finer daggers for words. Tears sprang to her eyes as she shrugged away from him. With Ian in her arms, she turned to face the father of her children, the man she was supposed to have wed, the very man who had seduced her and then locked her away.

Mistake?

His expression turned hard and as cold as steel. He sighed deeply. "I've a proposition."

Fiona suddenly couldn't speak past the knot in her throat. Taking comfort in Ian's soft coos, she held her son to her breast, and though the glitter in her eyes must have betrayed her, she lifted her chin. And yet...

6

nothing could have prepared her for what he was about to say.

"You may choose one of our sons," he said. "The other you must leave with me. If you agree to this, I will return Glen Abbey Manor to you and to your father."

Fiona blinked, disbelieving her ears. Whatever she had expected, it wasn't this. Her throat constricted and her mouth would not open to speak.

"I would allot you a generous allowance to comfortably raise *my* son."

"No!" She found her voice at last. "How can you possibly expect me to abandon my flesh and blood?"

He stood firm. "You have no choice in the matter."

"I refuse to leave either!"

"If you fight me," he warned, his tone colder than she'd ever heard it before, "I will take both and send you away with neither." He gave her no more than an instant to digest the threat and then added, "Nor will I return Glen Abbey Manor to your father. You will be homeless and childless besides."

Her heart seemed to plummet to her feet. Had she not been holding Ian she might have given in to a swoon. In desperation, she clutched her son to her breast. Pride vanished completely. "I'll stay," she said, choking back tears. "I'll do what you wish. Please, don't take my children!"

His voice hardened. "I'm afraid you've made it very clear to me that allowing you to remain in Meridian is an impossibility."

"But you... you cannot do this," she said, trembling. She shook her head in denial, but even as she did so, she knew he could, and he would do precisely as he wished. In his domain, Julian could do anything he pleased, and if it pleased him to send her away empty-handed, she knew that he could. Who would take him to task over it?

Nobody.

She was hardly important enough for anyone to raise their head over, much less their hand. The futility of it all swept through her as a terrible wave of nausea.

"Julian," she begged, and stumbled to her knees, clasping her son to her breast. Ian started to cry in earnest, sensing her distress, and she loosened her grip.

"You have one hour to choose which of our two sons you will take and to pack your belongings," he said, resolved. "I've already made arrangements for you to be escorted home."

"No—please!" Fiona begged.

Julian raised a hand to silence her, his jaw taut. His gaze lost every trace of warmth. "And if you return," he warned, "I shall take both my sons and leave you with nothing—not even your lofty pride."

Shock, for an instant, stopped the pounding of her heart. What pride was there in a woman on her knees? Fiona blinked away stinging tears.

Without another word, Julian turned and left her with the cold reality of his intentions. As the door closed behind him and the key turned in the lock, she vowed one day to make him pay. In the end she would have both her sons, and he would die a lonely old man.

CHAPTER 1

NORTHERN SCOTLAND, 1831

ho was she?
Misty woodlands enveloped them, forbidding even moonlight from illuminating their northward passage to a remote township in northern Scotland where J. Merrick Welbourne IV traveled in search of answers.

Resting his head against the window, he perused the unfamiliar countryside through a single open eye. Tonight the beaten road was peaceful, but the darkish woods made excellent spawning grounds for thieves and rogues. Like rats in the sewers of London, the north lands were said to be infested. Only a Tom O'Bedlam would venture through this place where brigands were said to thrive and townsfolk sheltered them, where outlanders were scrutinized through narrowed eyes.

Merrick had been forewarned, but he'd come anyway, bound for a place called Glen Abbey. His father's letters—dozens of them—had been penned to a woman who lived there. Though the letters had proven too vague to determine their relationship, it had become quite apparent by their sheer numbers that they'd been written to someone his father had once cared for.

Now he considered what he should do when—if—he found her, and he patted a hand over his coat where he'd put the stolen missive.

Should he deliver it?

Or should he, in truth, honor his father's wishes and let the past lie in peace?

For that matter, would she even accept this letter if he chose to deliver it?

The tone of the posts suggested that his father had somehow abused her. He wondered what terrible thing his father had done to this lady and was curious as to why the letters had never been dispatched. It was even more troubling that his father hardly left his apartments, reading these letters each and every night, sometimes weeping, and drinking himself into a stupor.

It was Merrick's greatest hope that he might find this woman and right an old wrong so that his father's conscience might somehow be eased. At the very least, he wanted answers...and answers he intended to get.

If ever they arrived at this mysterious little township. He felt as though he'd been traveling for years.

With a sigh, he slumped back into the leather seat, closing his eyes, seeking patience. The journey seemed bloody endless.

In truth, Merrick wasn't proud to have snooped like a petty thief through his father's personal correspondence, but he'd felt driven to discover what lay at the heart of his father's misery. It was his duty to his father as much as it was his duty to his country. It was a blessing that Meridian was not of particular importance politically, as there were no provisions in their laws that would depose a sovereign for dementia. That was the first amendment Merrick intended to make. If by chance he ended like his father, he wanted them to pluck him from his sovereignty quicker than he could blink, and to confer it at once to his heir.

Of course, in order to ascend to the throne, it also meant he must first get himself a wife—an ancient law he would sooner do away with. But for now, he must comply. And yet, the thought of that particular task sat like acid in his belly. He shook his head over the thought of all those silly little chits bouncing off their mothers' skirts. The prospect of having to make witty banter with empty-headed misses until he chose a bride made his stomach turn violently. The anticipation of having to endure one of them for the rest of his natural life gave him a fright. And their mothers—gad —vultures, every one! Depressing as the task might be, he was glad to have escaped London for the time being.

Somewhere beyond the carriage a bird call caught his attention and his eyes flew wide.

It was not merely any bird, but a saker—or to be more precise, a very good imitation. He'd know that sound anywhere.

He rapped on the carriage roof. "Did you hear that, Ryo?"

The driver's reply was petulant, as though he'd been stewing for the entire journey. "I hear nothing, Merricksan! I only do what I am told!"

Merrick frowned at the response—sour old codger. But Ryo's objections over Merrick's intervention wasn't his greatest concern at the moment. Unless his ears deceived him, he had, in fact, heard a saker's call. It was, after all, his favored bird of prey.

He'd been no more than twelve when Ryo first introduced him to the bold predator. And because it was more familiar to Oriental and Arab falconers, he'd never encountered anyone who'd owned one aside from himself. However, this was not the Orient, nor was it Meridian, and sakers didn't fly wild in the north woods of Scotland.

He sat forward, peering out the window.

Somehow the night seemed blacker than it should. Shadows teased his eyes, and, for an instant, he had the strangest perception of looking down over his carriage, sleek and black as it wheeled its way along the leaf-strewn path. The image was fleeting, gone before he had time to blink his eyes, but it was enough to make him doubt not only his vision but his hearing, as well.

He slumped backward, unsettled, his mood growing darker than the woods they traversed.

They should have reached Glen Abbey Manor long before now... If he didn't know better, he'd think Ryo was driving in circles, delaying their arrival.

He rapped again on the carriage roof. "Chrissakes, Ryo, get us to a bed—any bed will do by now!"

Ryo replied, "Grab your pants, Merricksan! We are going fast as we can."

"Not fast enough," Merrick suggested. "And that would be 'hold your knickers,'" he corrected the elder man, "not 'grab your pants.'"

"Same ting," the elder man argued from his perch outside.

"No," Merrick persisted, amused despite himself. "You would, in fact, find yourself in gaol for grabbing your pants in public."

Ryo's response was indignant. "Humph! Why should anybody care if I am grabbing my pants, but not if I am holding my knickers? Your Western language makes no sense to this old man."

Merrick refused to laugh, but his shoulders betrayed him, shaking softly with his mirth. Dammit all to hell, he was far too tired to be diverted. And he'd reduced himself to arguing semantics with a stubborn old

Asian, who somehow, despite his position of servitude, never once lost an argument.

Why the hell had he asked Ryo to drive, anyway? Or had Ryo insisted upon accompanying him?

Somehow, Merrick was never quite certain of these things where Ryo was concerned. If Merrick asked to dine on steak, the bugger served him raw fish instead. If he requested brandy, he got bloody ale. If he begged for silence, Ryo would sooner hum some lively tune, only to be contrary. This was their relationship, and though at times it bedeviled the hell out of Merrick, he wouldn't have it any other way.

At the instant, however, he was too tired to be anything but irritated. "God have pity," he muttered.

Despite claims to the contrary, Ryo's hearing was impeccable. The old man interjected without invitation, "Could be that Merricksan's discomfort is divine retribution for disrespecting his elders."

Merrick countered, "Could be Ryo would be better served by minding his own affairs."

Ryo didn't respond.

Wise old man. He seemed to know precisely when to launch an attack and precisely when to withdraw. Although he couldn't seem to resist a final kick of frustration to the carriage, Merrick noted. The impact of his foot rattled the vehicle.

Ornery old codger; let him show his temper. It didn't matter. Merrick was well armored in his conviction that he was doing his duty. Answers awaited him in Glen Abbey, and the devil and his hounds couldn't keep him from discovering what they were.

READY TO STRIKE when the leader gave word, seven men watched from their perches in the trees as the unfamiliar vehicle approached—for yet a third time. Dressed in black from head to heel, they allied with the night.

They needed this loot, but something about that particular carriage left the leader ill at ease. Unmarked though it might be, it was too well-heeled to leave itself so vulnerable. Either the occupant was foolish… and lost… else the carriage was bait… to catch a thief.

Cupping his hand over his mouth, Ian MacEwen made to call out the signal, but indecision froze his lips.

Twice before he'd let the carriage pass, but its returning presence was like a frosted pitcher of ale laid before a thirsty man. It didn't matter that it might be laced with poison, its sparkling contents were tempting beyond reason.

"God's bones. His direction's rotten as me minny's haggis," remarked one of his men.

"A week ago I'd 'a given the use of my cock for that haggis," remarked another, almost too softly to be heard.

But everyone heard.

What did one say to a man who'd lost his youngest daughter to a battle against hunger?

Three years old, Ana had been her name—sweet and shy, with little red curls and a button nose. Everyone understood why Rusty Broun was here tonight; he had three more little birds waiting at home with mouths open wide and bellies as empty as Glen Abbey's coffers.

"Trust me," Ian said to them, his heart squeezing as he weighed the options. And he knew they would. Trust him. They followed him blindly, consumed with hope.

Good men, every one, they'd leave this place if they could, but where would they go? To London to feed off sewer scraps?

Who in God's name would take them in with their wives and their bairns?

No, Ian had to do something.

But what to do?

Silence met his question, a weighted silence that trampled heavily over bracken, snapping twigs below.

The carriage was nearly upon them.

It was now or never…

Anticipation grew thick as the lowering fog.

As of yet they hadn't killed for loot—never intended to if they could help it—but tonight they might be forced to wield weapons if the approaching vehicle was a trap.

Someone could die.

And yet how many more children would die without their aid?

The image of little Ana's suffering, gaunt face spurred his decision once and for all, and he called out the signal for his men to strike. Let consequences fall where they may.

"Kiak-kiak-keiek-keiek!"

Within the instant, the carriage was beneath them. Ian was the first to descend. Drawing the black-hooded mask down over his face, as he went, landing cleanly atop the roof. Before the driver could shout a warning, he pressed his blade to the foreigner's throat.

THE CARRIAGE CAREENED TO A HALT. The jolt sent Merrick flying, with an oath spewing from his lips. His first thought was that Ryo had never been so belligerent, but clarity came to him at once. His long-time servant might be impertinent, but he was neither militant nor disrespectful.

Something was wrong.

His gut said brigands; the dark night invited them. Automatically, he unsheathed the blade he kept at his boot. If Ryo's life were not at risk, he would have spoken by now to alert Merrick, or at least to assuage him. Not a word came from that quarter and the trampling on the rooftop verified his suspicions. Outside, he discerned the sounds of men dropping from the trees—their landings crushing heavy twigs beneath their weight. Clearly, what he'd thought was Ryo's kick of frustration must have been one of them dropping directly atop the carriage.

God help them if they harmed Ryo, because Merrick would yank out their spines through their throats and make them spineless in truth. Crouching, prepared to defend himself, he waited for the carriage door to open. When at last it did, the masked thief seemed momentarily stunned by the sight of him. The fool froze where he stood, gaping into the carriage. Using the man's stupor to his advantage, he reared back and boxed the man in the jaw with the butt of his blade. The impact made Merrick wince, but he hadn't an instant to dwell on it. The thief recovered swiftly, flinging himself into the carriage as Ryo suddenly whipped the horses into flight. His weight drove Merrick backward as the carriage bolted forward. Flying from Merrick's grasp, the blade flung itself against the carriage roof then ricocheted to the floor, skimming Merrick's forehead on the way down. He struggled to retrieve it as a warm tide flooded into his eyes, but the thief caught his arms, pinning them. The man slammed his thick head against Merrick's face, and, for an instant, Merrick's vision faded. The roar of carriage wheels sounded like thunder in his ears. Shouts faded with every turn of the wheels.

"Stop!" the thief demanded.

Merrick thought he might be shouting at Ryo to halt the carriage, and silently praised Ryo's fearlessness.

Suddenly the thief reached up and snatched the hood from his head, unveiling himself to Merrick. To Merrick's utter shock, the face revealed to him was his own, and he froze where he lay, his vision going grey at the edges. Stupefied, he stared up into familiar eyes.

CHAPTER 2

"*M*y son is not so terrible," Lady Fiona said.

Perhaps it was in bad form to argue that point with a devoted mother, but Chloe Simon heartily disagreed.

Ian MacEwen, the fifth Earl of Lindale, was a pompous, spoiled, womanizing rogue, with a face God wasted on so frivolous a man. And Lady Fiona—God bless her—was blinded by a mother's love. It seemed to Chloe that, no matter the magnitude of his sins, her atrocious son could do no wrong. For Chloe's part, however, his latest discourtesy had, once and for all, relegated him to the realm of the unredeemable.

Something in her expression must have apprised Lady Fiona to her true sentiments, because Fiona rebuked her. "You mustn't be so overcritical, dear. A megrim is nothing to sneeze at."

Chloe tried not to screw her face. Megrim—humph! The milksop excused himself only to sneak out the back door. Chloe watched him depart with her own two eyes. She simply couldn't bring herself to relay that information to his doting mother. The self-indulgent sot couldn't even put his vices aside long enough to celebrate his mother's birthday. Instead of excusing himself with a megrim, he ought to have simply told her he didn't care. At least it would have been more honest.

Poor Lady Fiona; hers was a sad tale.

Most folks knew her father went about claiming his daughter was set to marry a prince. But Chloe's father had told her something entirely different. He said Lady Fiona fell in love with a commoner—a merchant, perhaps. She eloped without her father's blessings. But that, in itself, Chloe found eternally romantic—loving someone so desperately you'd risk everything for their love. Alas, the tale didn't end there. Less than a year after the couple had wed—away in some port town Chloe couldn't remember the name—Lady Fiona's husband was murdered on the docks. Left with a small bairn to care for, she'd written her papa with the news. The old earl loved his daughter, and though he'd felt she'd shamed him, he welcomed her home. But then, the tale only worsened; the earl died whilst Lady Fiona was en route home, and when she returned, she buried her father amidst gossip and whispers. The saddest part of all was that the earl never had the opportunity to meet his grandson. Perhaps Lord Lindale would have been a different man with the old earl's influence.

Wasn't it enough Lindale wasted every penny the estate earned? Must he show such blatant disregard for the woman who gave him birth?

No, he wasn't "so terrible," he was worse than terrible.

Unfeeling, self-indulgent oaf.

She intended to meet him at the back door to give him more than a piece of her mind. His actions were unforgivable.

She helped Lady Fiona into her bed.

"Chloe, dear," his mother persisted. "Ian has a good heart... you must endeavor to forgive him."

"Yes, I'm certain," Chloe said as pleasantly as she

TANYA ANNE CROSBY

was able, adding silently that she was quite certain he
had *none* at all.

Offering Lady Fiona a sympathetic smile, she
tucked the blankets about the sweet lady's limp legs,
trying to make her as comfortable as she was able.

"He simply doesn't know how to show it," Lady
Fiona persisted.

More like, he didn't know how to use his wicked
heart, Chloe countered, if only to herself. In truth, if
Lindale ever, even once in his life, allowed his heart to
guide him, Chloe would lick his dandy boots. She
simply wouldn't believe it. "Shall I find you a good
book to read," she asked gently, changing the subject.
"Or are you much too weary this eve?"

Lady Fiona waved her hand in dismissal, her kind
blue eyes glittering with… disappointment?

Chloe couldn't help it. She couldn't lie about her
feelings. She didn't like Lady Fiona's wayward son and
never had.

"Reading, my dear, is a pursuit better left for
younger eyes."

Chloe stood, squeezing Lady Fiona's hand, and said,
"You are not old!" She certainly didn't look it. At fifty-
six, Fiona was still quite beautiful, her skin as vibrant
and youthful as it had been the day Chloe first met her.
The shocking white in her hair was the only trait to betray her age. And even from the confines of her chair,
the set of her shoulders was even, revealing a lean waist
and a youthful frame.

Fiona squeezed her hand back, her delicate fingers
gripping with far more strength than it seemed possible she should possess in her deteriorated state.
"Humph!" she argued, her eyes glistening. "I'm crusty,
my dear, that's the truth!"

Her inelegant description of herself brought a reluctant smile to Chloe's lips. Nothing could be further

from the truth; Lady Fiona had more elegance in her small finger than most women possessed in their entire bodies.

"Then I should bid you good night," Chloe said, and left the lady's bedside to put out the lamp on the dresser. "Happy birthday," she said.

"No," said Fiona, waving Chloe away from the lamp. "Please leave it. It will go out on its own."

Chloe twisted her lips. It was dangerous to leave lamps burning all night long, but Fiona seemed fearful of the dark. "As you wish, my lady."

"Chloe, dear, will you kindly stop addressing me so formally," Lady Fiona rebuked. "You *must* call me Fiona. I consider you family. Have I not made you welcome?"

"Oh, yes!" Chloe replied. "Very much so."

Lady Fiona gave her an admonishing look, but said dismissively, "Good night, dear."

"Sweet dreams," said Chloe, and she left the room, pulling the door gently closed behind her. Later, after giving Lord Lindale a bit of the devil, she would return to put out the lamp. It really wasn't any trouble. But she sighed wearily, loathing the thought of tangling with Fiona's son.

God only knew, Lindale didn't deserve the respect of his peers, much less his mother's—and certainly not hers! Chloe couldn't bear to address him by his title, except with the contempt he deserved. The old lairds would surely turn in their graves because Ian was an utter disgrace to the MacEwen name.

PAIN WAS Merrick's first awareness.

Voices surrounded him.

Shadows flitted past his heavy lids.

"Hawk?"

TANYA ANNE CROSBY

"Is 'e dead?"

"No, y' arse! Canna ye hear him moaning like a wee one?"

Merrick opened his eyes to find strange faces peering down at him—faces with hoods drawn back and even a few missing teeth. At first he thought he might be dreaming, so hazy was his vision. It took him a groggy instant to realize that he lay on the cold ground and that the bodies that belonged to the disembodied faces hovering over him were half cloaked in a bone-dampening fog.

"He's coming aboot!" said one of the men excitedly.

"Are ye a'right, Hawk?" asked another.

"Damn!" Merrick said, and shook his head, trying to clear his vision. He tried to rise, but fell backward on his arse.

"Bloody bastard. He left ye here to rot," said the man.

Yet another man stepped forward, throwing his hood back as he offered Merrick a grimy hand. Even with his impaired vision, he spied black dirt beneath the nails.

Pride warred with good sense. He could bloody well get to his own feet without assistance from the enemy. Ignoring the outstretched hand, he struggled to his feet.

"Sorry, Hawk. There was naught we could do," the first man explained.

Merrick frowned. Why did they keep calling him Hawk? Couldn't they bloody well see who he was?

Reaching up to feel for a wound at his head, he discovered a hood covering his face. Christ be damned!

No wonder he wasn't seeing straight! He snatched off the hood, glaring at the men surrounding him, expecting them to apologize for the confusion—a more motley crew he'd never met. Cursing, he tossed the bloodied hood away. But a downward glance revealed himself dressed in strange clothing, as well. Instinctively his hand went to his head where he found his forehead sticky. The tinny scent of his own blood stung his nostrils.

"Where's that slimy bastard?" he demanded of the moron who'd extended his hand. At the instant he wanted only to wrap his hands about the robber's throat and squeeze.

And where was Ryo?

"He got away," the toothless man declared.

Merrick's brain was so muddled he forgot he'd asked a question to begin with. "Who?"

The toothless man's brows collided as he answered, "The slimy bastard," he said. "You asked where he'd gone." His head tilted and his expression was unmistakably one of concern. "Dinna ye recall anythin' at all, Hawk?"

No. Dammit. The last thing he remembered was refusing to answer that thug's questions. He'd demanded his own answers, but the man whacked him on the noggin instead. That was the last of his memory.

"Bloody driver took off during the scuffle," the taller man said. "We tried to follow..."

"By the time we got the horses," another interjected, "you were gone."

The veins at Merrick's temples throbbed. If someone had warned him yesterday that he'd be robbed by a bandit who looked enough like him to be his twin, and that he'd be stuck at the mercy of his bumbling men while the thief made away with his carriage, he'd have believed it a jest. But there was nothing amusing about this situation, and the laughter that burst from his throat was manic.

The men all stared at him, befuddled.

He counted them—six—six ruffians against one. He was no match for these men, no matter what idiots they might be. He couldn't defeat so many—weapon-less, to boot.

Merrick's laughter stopped abruptly. Dizzied by his outburst, he took a step and nearly fell.

"Ye dinna look so well, Hawk. We should take you home."

Merrick opened his mouth to speak but the man interjected very quickly. "I know ye dinna think it wise to be seen together, but I canna allow ye to stumble home in this condition."

What bloody condition was that?

And where the hell was home?

"We'll tell 'em you took a fall from your horse," he said, fumbling for a story. "And... yes... we'll tell them we came across you on the road and offered to see ye home." He nodded. "That's what we'll say." And then to the others, he added, "Go on home, lads. I'll see to this myself. It wouldn't look good if we went there together."

Where was there?

Evidently, they'd mistaken his identity. Merrick decided it might not be wise to enlighten them just yet.

At any rate, *home* sounded damned good at the instant, no matter whose home it might be. He slipped off the ring that bore Meridian's royal crest and pocketed it. He was tired, in pain, probably bleeding to death, and lost besides—not to mention intensely curious about his nemesis.

He nodded, overcome by the situation. "Very well, then, lead the way."

CHLOE TRIED, but couldn't get little Ana's face out of her head—that poor, sweet child—God rest her soul. Chloe had struggled to save her, but she had simply lost the will to live. She understood now how her father must have suffered over the loss of every patient.

Pacing the hall as she awaited Lindale's return, she stopped to cast malevolent glances out the window. Truth be told, she'd awaited this moment a long time, biding her time, minding her tongue.

No longer.

And the more she paced, the angrier she got.

What sort of man passed a hungry child on the street, ignored her outstretched arms, and spent his money on women and drink instead?

What sort of man took a father's last coin, when his child lay suffering on her deathbed?

What sort of man stole a young girl's home, and her dreams, when her da was fresh in his grave?

Ian MacEwen was that man. And though it might seem irreverent of her, Chloe wasn't inclined to wait on God to see justice done. It was no longer a matter of what he'd done to her; he was out there, destroying innocent lives. Somehow, she swore, she was going to see that he paid for his sins.

Hearing voices at long last, she raced to the window and thrust aside the silk draperies. They were so ancient they were brittle in her grasp, and she looked at them in disgust, wondering where all the money went —not for the upkeep of this house or its mistress, that much was certain!

Riders approached. Chloe recognized both men at once. Escorted by Rusty Brown, Lindale wobbled in his saddle like a common pub brawler. So furious that she didn't care who witnessed her tirade, she lifted up her skirts and marched toward the door, determined to let the entire world know what sort of man the lord of Glen Abbey Manor was.

HOME, he thought. Modest, but sprawling, even if it appeared as though it hadn't been cared for in a score of years. Eager to get back onto his own two feet, he never anticipated the welcome they received.

They'd given him Hawk's mount and he'd insisted upon riding though he could scarcely remain in the saddle. His head throbbed and he was dizzy and sick to his belly besides. He tried to listen to every word of his escort's prattling, storing away details for later. In the morning he fully intended to see these men were arrested.

Clearly, "Hawk" was their leader, but that particular fact didn't surprise Merrick much. What did surprise him was the regard with which Rusty seemed to address him. The man seemed determined to instruct him in what to say and how to behave once they reached, of all places, Glen Abbey Manor.

And now his curiosity was more than roused.

It might've been mere coincidence that Hawk looked so much like him he could have been his twin, but that he resided at Glen Abbey Manor, as well? The former was remarkable, the latter suspect. Unfortunately, he didn't have time to consider the possibilities. No sooner had they ridden onto the lawn when they were accosted by screaming servants—or perhaps it was only a single woman. The ungodly sound she made was like a banshee shrieking into his ears. He tried to dismount, but his vision skewed. Misjudging the distance to the ground, he tumbled from the saddle into lean, but strong arms.

Bloody hell, his injuries must have been fatal because he found himself coddled at the bosom of the loveliest angel.

The scent of roses enveloped him in a sensual cocoon. Delicate hands pressed his cheek against velvety breasts, while a face as beautiful as heaven itself peered down upon him. For the first time in all his life J. Merrick Welbourne IV was speechless at the sight of a woman. If he wasn't dead, then surely he must be dreaming.

And then his angel shouted at him and he knew he wasn't dreaming. She was flesh-and-blood woman, and he wanted suddenly to kiss her... until her words penetrated the fog in his brain, and he realized what she was saying.

"It serves the wretch right!" she declared, her breasts rising with indignation. "I don't believe he is hurt for one minute. He's merely too muddled to ride. Rotten cad!"

"Nay, Miss Chloe! His horse threw him—I swear! We saw it with our own two eyes!"

"Who is 'we'?" she questioned.

Bloody shrew; she must be Hawk's wife.

"Och!" she snapped before Merrick could ask who she was. "He's bleeding all over my dress!" And she promptly dropped Merrick to the ground. He landed with a sickening thud that rattled his brain. Once again, his head clouded with pain, and the last thing he remembered was the fuzzy image of her standing over him, examining her ruined dress, and the sound of her irate voice cursing the day he was born.

And then he did what no manly man should ever do; he swooned.

CHAPTER 3

*C*hloe was employed to nurse Lady Fiona, not her wretched son. But it seemed more and more, even without this latest incident, that Lady Fiona charged her with some task that involved Lord Lindale.

It nettled her.

He nettled her.

Rotten knave.

Forced to nurse him throughout the night, while Lady Fiona sat, looking on from her invalid chair, she assured his fretting mother, "He'll be fine. Don't you worry." She tried hard not to sound so heartless, but there simply wasn't a bone in her body that felt pity for the cur. Clearly, he wasn't drunk—not this time, but she still resented having to care for him. Nor did it change the fact that he'd abandoned his mother on her birthday, only to go out carousing.

He lay in his bed, sleeping more peacefully than he had any right to. Chloe feared he'd cracked his skull— but the gash on his forehead was superficial, needing only two wee stitches. He'd bear a scar, but so far as Chloe was concerned, it was his just due. The wicked should bear a wicked countenance.

Certainly, it didn't seem fitting that Lucifer should

be the loveliest angel, though in studying Lord Lindale's slumbering face, she could well believe that to be true. But the thought made her frown, because she didn't like to admit that his countenance appealed to her.

His face bore the same chiseled look of his ancestors depicted in Glen Abbey Manor's gallery. His hair was a dark, sun-kissed blond. Shaded slightly darker by moisture from her cloth, it was brushed away from his face, revealing magnificently high cheekbones and a strong jaw shadowed with shimmering gold whiskers.

Pursing her lips, she studied the gold flakes. Odd, but she thought she remembered him clean-shaven this afternoon. But it must have been her imagination.

Very gingerly examining the new stitches on his forehead, admiring her handiwork, she turned her attention once more to his face. In stark contrast to his masculine features, his lips were full and his lashes thick and dark against his rosy cheeks. Most women would die for such lashes. And he must have inherited his father's complexion, she decided, because Fiona was considerably fairer. Of course, Chloe wouldn't know, because she'd never met Ian's father, nor did his portrait grace Glen Abbey's gallery.

"He looks pallid," worried Lady Fiona.

"He's fine," Chloe assured, though he did, in fact, seem a little peculiar. As she mopped about his forehead, trying to put her finger on the distinction, Edward, Glen Abbey's long-time steward, entered the room and whispered something into Lady Fiona's ear.

Chloe didn't bother to greet the man. He wouldn't acknowledge her anyway. Like Lord Lindale, Glen Abbey's steward didn't seem to condone her presence at the Manor. *Too bad.* Chloe didn't particularly like him, either. He was secretive and abrasive and seemed to have far too much sway over Lady Fiona.

Lady Fiona gasped. "The constable, you say?"

"Yes, madame," Edward said darkly.

"Whatever for?"

"He did not say, madame, but I believe he wishes to speak with lord Lindale."

"How rude!" Lady Fiona declared, her mettle peeking out from behind her elegant facade. Chloe had often thought she should have been born a queen, not merely an earl's daughter. "He certainly may not!" Clearly unsettled, Lady Fiona's voice trembled slightly. "You may inform him that he must return at a decent hour when my son has had ample opportunity to recover."

Edward bent once more to whisper something Chloe couldn't quite make out, and Lady Fiona replied, "Well, then! Take me to him at once. I shall tell him myself!"

"Yes, madame," Edward replied, and he complied at once, wheeling Lady Fiona out from the room. The cumbersome chair scraped the door on the way out.

"Lord-a-mercy, Edward! Are you trying to kill me?" she complained.

"Of course not, madame. I beg your pardon."

They left Chloe smiling to herself. Even in her condition, Lady Fiona's mettle was an inspiration.

Now, alone with her charge, and with Lady Fiona and Edward certain not to return for a while, she allowed herself to admire the contour of Lindale's body beneath the sheets. His chest was wide, his limbs long and muscular. He was nearly bare, she knew. They'd removed his shirt. And, no, it wasn't the first time she'd seen a man unclothed—she'd nursed more than a few— but it was certainly the first time she'd been alone with this man. Casting a glance over her shoulder, she lifted one corner of his blanket to peer beneath—in the interest of science, of course.

SEDUCED BY A PRINCE

Really, it wasn't as though he would ever know; he was fast asleep.

Her heart beat a little faster as she lifted the coverlet. A sprinkling of curly hair beckoned to her touch, but Chloe wouldn't dare. It began at his chest, tapering to a fine, silky line that drew her gaze still lower, even despite her sense of propriety. He was, indeed, a beautiful specimen of a man. She was loath to admit that. His tawny flesh stretched taut over such beautiful muscles, but she didn't remember his skin being so dark.

Her heart skipped a beat as she contemplated lifting the cover a little higher to peer a bit lower—not that she would see much more. He was still wearing his trousers, but what a terrible waste of a man, she thought with disgust.

MERRICK LAY STILL AS STONE, in no rush to awake.

He couldn't recall the last time he'd felt a woman's nurturing touch—nor even the first time, for that matter. He'd had lovers aplenty, but this was somehow different.

As a child, it was Ryo who'd cared for him when he was ill, and Ryo who'd reared him to manhood. Strength and honor had been instilled in him from the day of his birth, though he very much feared that behind his mask, he was no more than an ordinary boy who craved a mother's love. It was never more apparent than it was this instant; he could have languished in the moment, never waking.

Her warm, sweet breath brushed his face and he turned toward it like a flower to the sun.

When he opened his eyes at last, it was to find *her* bent over him, her face near his chest as she peeked beneath his covers, ogling him. Her private smile was the most sensuous thing he had ever witnessed. It stirred his loins, rousing the one part of him that didn't ache—at least not at this very instant. Her lips curved softly, admiringly, and he feared that if she didn't drop those covers at once, she would witness, firsthand, the prompt erection of a royal tent.

As a matter of self-preservation, he spoke. But he couldn't keep himself from baiting her. "Enjoying the view?"

She dropped the coverlet with a startled gasp.

He watched as a flush crept from the valley of her breasts, tinting her face. Her lips deepened to rose, and he wondered if they would be warm to the touch... hot and soft.

Bloody hell. Not for the first time, he had the most overwhelming urge to kiss her.

Recovering her composure quickly, his dubious angel tossed the wet cloth she held over his face, as though to escape his knowing gaze. "Oh!" she exclaimed. "You're awake!" Though her color betrayed her, her tone was full of irritation.

"I am," Merrick assured, removing the damp cloth from his face. He smiled disarmingly—at least he thought it should be disarming, but she seemed entirely unaffected.

"More's the pity," she lamented. "It appears not even the devil wants you, *my lord.*"

Her contemptuous tone didn't escape him.

Grimacing, Merrick adjusted himself on the bed to give her better access. "What," he taunted her, "no welcome-home kiss for your darling husband?"

He had no idea where the question came from, only that it spilled too easily from his lips.

She gasped, aloud, as though offended by his quip, and then she took a defensive step backward. "How dare you speak to me as you would one of your strumpets! That fall must have addled your limited little brain!"

But she didn't answer his question: who was she, dammit?

And then she added too glibly, "I shall inform your mother you have awakened, my lord—just in time for company! The constable will be quite pleased not to have to wait, after all." Whirling about, she meant to take her leave.

"Rusty lied," he said before she could walk out. "It wasn't a fall."

She stopped abruptly, her curiosity piqued.

That waist—so tiny his hands could easily span it. She turned slowly to face him.

Merrick weighed his words; he was hoping for an ally, but wasn't certain how much to reveal. "The horse didn't throw me," he confessed.

One delicate brow arched. "Really?"

"I was, in fact, robbed," he said.

Both her brows lifted now. "Really!" she said again, her face suddenly losing its animosity. In truth, she appeared rather hopeful.

Merrick nodded, watching her closely. "Indeed."

She took a step closer. "Was it Hawk?" she asked, and the tone of her voice was suddenly awestruck.

Merrick stared at her, disbelieving. She lived with the rotten thief and didn't realize who he was? "Yes," he said tersely, deciding that Hawk obviously never shared his secret with his lovely wife.

She was somebody else's woman.

He was struck, on the heels of that revelation, with a wave of envy as foreign to him as the bed in which he lay.

Chrissakes, when in his life had he ever envied anyone anything? His entire life he'd had everything at his disposal simply for the taking.

She straightened to her full height and seemed to be assessing him. "I don't believe you," she said suddenly.

"Why not?"

"Because." Her expression was smug now. "You should be so fortunate to exchange even glances with that man. You aren't fit to wipe his boots. That you breathe the same air is a blasphemy in itself."

Merrick blinked at her declarations.

Two things struck him in that instant. One, she had absolutely no notion of her connection with the inestimable Hawk. And two, she didn't seem to like her own husband very much.

In fact, he'd like to have wholeheartedly agreed with her assessment of Lindale, but her accusations seemed somewhat more personal than they should have been, considering that she wasn't even talking about Merrick. She was talking about Lindale—who was, in fact, Hawk. Be damned if the madness of the situation didn't entirely amuse him, even despite that her vehemence was directed, for the moment, squarely at him. "Is that so?" he asked wryly.

"Yes, of course. He is everything you are not."

Slack-jawed, Merrick sat, not bothering to cover his bare chest. Why trouble himself? She'd already had an eyeful.

She gasped at the sight of him, and turned to go, suddenly and conveniently embarrassed by the sight of him.

"And what is it that I am?" he asked, baiting her. He didn't want her to leave just yet.

She turned to face him again, clearly far too tempted by the opportunity to gut him, and lifting a hand to her face, covering her eyes as she spoke. But the flush in her breast returned, followed by the one in her cheeks. And yet, she didn't cow. Her mettle brought a smile to Merrick's lips. "I shall be most pleased to make you a list," she apprised him, and then added, "After you do me the courtesy of covering yourself, Lord Lindale."

He ignored her request. "Make me a list," he dared.

"Are you decent?"

More so than he'd like to be. "No."

"Why not?"

"Because I warrant tis nothing you haven't seen numerous times before," he told her quite pointedly, and waited for her to deny it.

She parted two fingers only slightly, peeking through, then closed them again with a soft gasp. "You are so crude!"

"Crude?" And yet, she didn't deny his allegation.

"And rude!" she added, but she didn't turn to leave, he noticed. In fact, he thought he saw her peek yet again through those long, delicate fingers—fingers that had touched him only moments before.

"Go on," he encouraged. As a test to see if she was looking, he let the coverlet fall further.

She gasped softly and his smile deepened. "I should say you are selfish, arrogant, spoiled, ungrateful, vulgar —shall I continue, my lord?"

"No, I think I get the idea," he relented, but with a smile.

"Yes, well, now, I am leaving," she informed him tersely. "Because I cannot bear to remain in your presence yet another instant, my lord!"

"What about Hawk?" he asked, his lips tipping upward when she made no move to leave.

"Hawk?" She sighed audibly, making him frown. "Well, of course, he is beloved, kind, compassionate, generous, charitable, noble, brave—"

With every endearing adjective, she lost a note of shrewishness; her tone becoming even wistful.

Merrick's smile vanished completely. "I thought you

were leaving," he said. Her defense of the bugger irritated him more than it should have.

"I *am* leaving," she assured.

"If you must know, he is nothing but a common thief," Merrick told her. "There is absolutely nothing noble about the man. He robbed me and left me to die where I lay."

He thought she rolled her eyes, but they were still covered, and he couldn't tell. "You were hardly in danger of bleeding to death," she assured, unmoved. "It was only a scratch."

"Really?" His fingers sought his wound for validation. "Scratches don't require stitching," he protested.

Damn, but was he looking for pity? He didn't deserve the contempt she was giving him.

Hawk did.

"Oh, yes, it should scar quite nicely," she said, sounding smug as she turned her back to him at last.

Heartless vixen.

"And so long as we are discussing the matter so freely," she added, casting him a dark glare over her shoulder, "I believe justice was served last night—a lesson to you for running out so rudely on your mother's birthday celebration. Now, if you will excuse me, Lord Lindale, I shall go and inform the constable you are eager to see him."

His mother's birthday celebration?

Her declaration rendered him speechless.

As though his eyes were drawn to it, he peered across the room, noticing for the first time the portrait of a woman in her youth. It was the same woman in the portrait his father guarded so fiercely. She was unmistakable in her elegance. He blinked, glancing back at the fiery angel paused in the doorway, and was struck at once by the truth.

It was no accident of nature that he and Hawk

looked so remarkably alike that no one seemed able to tell them apart.

Pure emotion barreled through him, the force of it so intense that he was relieved he was lying down. He opened his mouth to speak, but no words came.

His angel marched from the room, leaving him to stare after her, stunned by his epiphany.

Hawk was his brother.

And his mother... she was... *alive*.

Ryo had known, damn the man to hell. That's why he'd tried so hard to keep Merrick from going to Glen Abbey Manor. It was also why he'd delayed their arrival as long as he'd dared and then bolted away at the first opportunity... probably thinking Merrick was still aboard, no doubt. He was like to be halfway to London by now... with his brother in tow.

When the haze cleared from Merrick's thoughts and he looked up again, his fiery angel was gone.

Leaping from the bed, he called, "Wait!" But he didn't know her bloody name and she didn't stop.

CHAPTER 4

*H*ow dare he look at her as though she'd rent his heart from his breast! Chloe seethed as she made her way to the drawing room, vexed with herself for feeling remorse where Lord Lindale was concerned. Why should she regret harsh words when he deserved to feel wretched?

In the drawing room she discovered Lady Fiona engaged in a heated discussion with Constable Tolly, refusing to give quarter. She smiled softly as she watched the mistress of Glen Abbey Manor at work. She guarded her privacy and her son like a lioness. And despite her threats to the contrary, she would no more betray Lord Lindale's state than she would ever betray Lady Fiona.

"My son will be most pleased to receive you on the morrow," she assured the constable. "However, today I shall not allow it." When he opened his mouth to protest, she said, "Please forgive me if you feel thwarted. That is not my intention. However, my son's wellbeing is my utmost concern at the instant. Tomorrow," she apprised him again.

The constable stood with his hat in hand, his face florid with agitation. "My lady," he pleaded. "How will I capture this brigand if you and the rest of Glen Abbey refuse to cooperate? You above all in this town should be most concerned after what he has done to you."

He was referring to her crippled legs, and he straightened uncomfortably, rising to his full height, clearly chagrined over having to mention it.

To no one's surprise, his awkward attempt to cow Fiona failed miserably. She was as unrelenting as the constable was persistent.

Unable to rise to the occasion, Lady Fiona straightened in her chair, clearly agitated. "Rest assured, it is my full intention to cooperate with your investigation, William. As you recall, I gave you a full report when I encountered the cad myself. But I simply cannot allow you to disturb my son whilst he recovers, and that is that!"

"But, madame!" the constable protested still. "The time to debrief Lord Lindale is now, while the incident is freshly impressed upon his brain. Not later, when time has eaten away at his memory like maggots."

"I beg of you, do not be so melodramatic!" Lady Fiona charged him. Her usually pale complexion bloomed as her fury rose. "And by the by, what incident is it you are speaking of?" she asked him, tapping her nails firmly against her wheeled chair. "I was told my son fell off his bloody horse!"

The constable gasped at her blasphemy. Lady Fiona never lost her sense of propriety. Still, he persisted. "*Attempted* robbery, my lady. We have reason to believe there may have been one."

"Really?" Chloe asked, lifting her brows. "Did someone report a robbery?"

The constable finally noticed her standing in the doorway. For an instant he considered his answer.

"Not precisely, Miss Chloe, but last evening there were reports of a strange vehicle in the area—headed toward Glen Abbey Manor. Today that vehicle seems to have utterly vanished. It obviously did not arrive at its destination, nor was it registered at the inn."

Chloe chewed her bottom lip, contemplating whether to reveal Lord Lindale's confession.

"I rather hoped Lord Lindale might shed some light on the mystery."

"What leads you to believe the carriage was bound for Glen Abbey Manor?" Chloe asked.

"Miss Chloe," he said impatiently. "No one ventures this way anymore unless they are bound for Glen Abbey Manor. It is the only estate left of any consequence."

"I see," Chloe said. That was true. Thanks to Lord Lindale's avarice, Glen Abbey was, indeed, a withering township. Too far inland to serve as a port town, and nearly inaccessible by land, the town had far too few resources, very little industry and a landlord who was intent upon collecting and spending every last farthing from his tenants.

The constable pleaded, "I beg you, Lady Fiona... that brigand is the very 'seed of corruption.'"

"Please, William," Lady Fiona said, rolling her eyes. "Spare us the theatrics."

Chloe tried not to smirk. It was no wonder the constable felt frustrated; his sentiments were hardly shared by the townsfolk here. And knowing that Hawk's efforts brought food to the mouths of babes, Chloe held her tongue.

If Lord Lindale wished to speak against Hawk, he would need do so himself.

Lady Fiona stood her ground. "I never said we would not cooperate, Constable. I only appeal to your sense of decency. Come back *tomorrow!*"

The constable was by now apoplectic. "Very well, you leave me no choice." He smashed the derby upon his head. "Good day!" he said smartly, and spun on his heels toward the door. "Good day to you, Miss Chloe." Taking his leave of the drawing room, he paused in the foyer to speak briefly with Edward. Chloe watched them with great interest, wondering when those two had become so friendly.

"I have absolutely fizzled," Lady Fiona said, turning Chloe's attention from the low-speaking pair at the door. "I believe I shall take myself out to the garden to enjoy the remainder of my morning."

"Yes, madame," Chloe said, still distracted by the pair at the door. Edward had been Lady Fiona's shadow since Chloe could recall... at least, until Chloe came to attend her. Ever since Chloe's arrival, Edward seemed far more inclined to his own pursuits. She took the helm of the invalid chair and maneuvered Fiona out of the room, taking her out the back.

The wheeled chair was a cumbersome contraption. Once outside, they struggled over steppingstones and patches of weed, which seemed to have sprung forth overnight. The chair caught at every pebble. As they encountered clumps of weeds, Chloe bent to yank them out from the ground, tossing them away from the stone path.

"You shouldn't have to do that," Lady Fiona said apologetically. But someone had to. Glen Abbey's only gardener had a long enough list of duties. The poor man struggled to fulfill them and to feed his family with only meager pay.

"I really don't mind," Chloe assured her. And she truly didn't. God gave her two hands to use. And besides, her mother had often labored, by choice, in their little garden at home, coaxing flowers to bloom. Chloe desperately missed the scent of freshly cut blossoms.

More than that, she missed her mother.

Reaching back to pat her hand, Fiona said, "You are

a godsend, my dear. Whatever would I do without you?"

"You would cow these pesky weeds into lying down for you," Chloe said as she pushed the wheeled chair toward Lady Fiona's favorite spot beneath the rose canopy. "I mean to say, not even Mother Nature would dare challenge you."

Fiona laughed softly, the sound almost musical. "Oh, but my dear, you don't seem the least bit cowed. I must be losing my touch."

Chloe smiled. Hardly, she thought, remembering the constable's florid complexion. Even from her invalid chair, Lady Fiona managed to make one feel as though she towered over them. She was kindhearted, but strong-willed. And she was reticent, in truth, but with more of an air of melancholy than one of bitterness. Chloe tried to remember the first time she'd met Lady Fiona and smiled, because she couldn't recall a time this lady wasn't part of her life. Like a long-reigning monarch, it seemed she had always been there. In better days, Lady Fiona had, in fact, been somewhat affectionately known as the queen of Glen Abbey.

They reached the rose canopy and Chloe settled her chair beneath the cascading rose vines so that she was free of the sun. She cast a glance in the direction of the house to be certain Edward had not followed and said, "I wanted to tell you while we were in the drawing room, but my lord is awake."

"God be praised!" she said, and Chloe didn't miss the note of relief.

IT WAS AN OLD HOUSE.

Taking care to avoid another confrontation before

42

he was ready for it, Merrick wandered the halls, taking in the deteriorated state of the manor.

At one time it must have been grand—nothing like the opulence of Meridian's palace, but noble, nonetheless.

More than he recalled at first glance, it was evident that no one made reparations for it now. And yet, though the walls were dingy, and the draperies were brittle and yellowed, every room he passed was immaculate.

Had they no funds to pay for the upkeep of this house? That seemed odd, considering the riches his father hoarded.

Alas, he'd encountered few servants along the way, but the ones in residence obviously gave their mistress their blood and sweat. Did they do so out of love?

Or did she bleed them like a leech?

The latter was easier to believe, because his flesh-and-blood mother must have been heartless to abandon her own babe.

He stopped to examine a portrait that hung at the head of the stairwell. If he didn't know better, he would swear he was looking at himself. But it was the present Lord Lindale, dressed in a deep blue waistcoat and a white, elaborately fashioned cravat—a bit dandyish for Merrick's taste. The tailcoat, however, was black—better, he supposed. Aside from the bright waistcoat, it could have been Merrick down to the last fine detail.

Obviously, he and 'Ian' were twins. He'd already concluded that much, but what he didn't know yet was how it came to be that he was foisted upon his father's wife. It would certainly explain the emotional detachment she'd kept toward him, never affording him a mother's care. Only what would she have had to gain by her silence?

Had his father threatened her? Bribed her?

Then again, she'd never born his father any issue. Perhaps raising a bastard hadn't been a concern for her since she hadn't had a son of her own who could inherit.

Merrick stared at the smirking portrait, trying to read the uncanny blue eyes. They were the same odd shade as his own. Only it had never struck him until this moment just how startling they were. A lover had once told him they were his most disquieting trait, because they always seemed to *know*.

How much did Ian know?

His brother certainly recovered his surprise quickly enough to steal Merrick's carriage, his clothes and life. Unfortunately, Merrick no longer even had the letter addressed to Fiona; it was in his vest pocket.

For better or worse, his twin was now in possession of it, and Merrick had only his face as proof of their kinship—startling enough as it was.

An incredible surge of anger pummeled through him.

Why, in God's name, had his father not accepted both his sons? More importantly, why had his mother agreed to leave one behind? Or had she any choice in the matter?

Perhaps she hadn't, and that would be the obvious source of his father's unremitting guilt. But what, precisely, did he regret? What did he do to this woman. Alas, it seemed the more Merrick uncovered, the more questions arose.

He wiped a finger across the framework of the portrait, found it free of dust and continued on down the hall toward Ian's room. There would be plenty of time to face his *mother*. He didn't yet know what to say to her. What did one say to the woman who'd abandoned you?

CHLOE KNOCKED FIRST upon Lord Lindale's door.

He, not Hawk, was the reason for Glen Abbey's decline. God help her, if she hadn't been in such dire straits after her father's death, she would never have agreed to suffer his employ. She could scarcely bear to look him in the face.

How could he face her after robbing her of her life? Moreover, how could he throw stones at Hawk when he was far worse than Hawk could ever be? Hawk stole to help others; Lindale stole out of greed.

What the old earl gave in friendship, the present earl snatched away without regret. And what was most unforgivable was that he'd done so at the blackest hour in Chloe's life—whilst she was burying her father. That afternoon, thieves overturned their cottage and stole every document her father had locked away—including the deed to their land and house, a gift from the old earl to her father for his years of loyal service. The thieves left everything else of value behind, which told Chloe that there was only one thing they were after.

She came to Glen Abbey Manor hoping to find proof. As yet, she'd found little more than a meddlesome steward who never seemed to sleep. What Chloe couldn't determine was whether the steward was merely watchful of his mistress or whether he was a minion of Lord Lindale's. In either case, the two seemed eternally at daggers drawn.

She knocked again, calling out to Lindale impatiently. When there was no answer, she opened his door to find the room empty. The disheveled state of his quarters startled her. The bedsheets were strewn across the floor, as though they'd been wrenched in a hurry from the bed. The entire room was in shambles, with clothes tossed everywhere and the wardrobe open wide... as though someone had been searching. It brought back memories of that terrible afternoon and set her teeth on edge.

But why would Lord Lindale feel the need to rifle through his own belongings? If there was one thing she knew about the man, it was that he was meticulous. Like a miser guarding his hoard, he knew where everything was at every moment.

Preoccupied with those thoughts, she turned to go, and her heart leaped a little to find him standing right behind her, watching. Her hand flew to her breast. She hadn't even heard him enter. "What are you doing here?"

He glowered at her and said very pointedly, "This is my room, is it not?"

Why did the quip seem more an inquiry than his usual sarcasm? Chloe furrowed her brow. "Of course," she answered. "I was... I mean to say, I didn't see you when I came in."

"I was out."

Something about his gaze was even darker, far more menacing than ever before. In fact, his demeanor seemed entirely different today. He'd donned familiar garments, but somehow he seemed to be wearing them differently—perhaps more elegantly and less... vainly.

"Where is my mother?" he asked, his tone hard.

"In the garden," Chloe replied. "Is something wrong?"

MERRICK CLENCHED HIS JAW.

Every bloody thing was wrong.

A fury of emotions warred within him. This might not be his life he was faced with, but neither was the one he'd left behind. As he'd watched her survey the di-

46

sheveled room, it occurred to him that his entire life had been a lie.

She was watching him warily, as though she sensed a difference in him. Well, he *was* different. It would behoove him to let her think the bump on his head caused him a lapse in memory. He still hadn't the first notion what his little shrew's name was, much less her relation to him. But one thing was certain: judging by the way she'd explored his body whilst he'd slept, she wasn't his sister. That conclusion filled him with a strange sense of relief.

She was, in truth, the most appealing woman he'd ever met. But he didn't know whether it was the natural bloom in those high cheeks that intrigued him, or those eyes that seemed to veil deep, earthy secrets. She was nothing at all like the coy debutantes he'd encountered in London. In fact, she was nothing like anyone he'd ever met. She had color in her face like a commoner unafraid of the sun's sweet kiss, but she was genteel and carried herself as regally as a princess.

Who was she?

The question plagued him.

"I was perusing the gallery," Merrick said carefully, watching her expressions. "Was your portrait never commissioned?"

She cocked her head, clearly bemused by his question. "Why should mine have been commissioned?"

Determined to discover their relation, he took a step toward her.

She took a step backward. "Are you feeling quite all right?" she asked.

He followed her again. "Quite," he reassured.

Her eyes narrowed, head tilted, she retreated yet another step and found her back against the dresser.

Merrick moved to trap her between his arms, leaning into the dresser and looking directly into her beautiful brown eyes. There was no fear there, he realized, only confusion. Her back was straight, and her chin tipped slightly upward—in defiance?

"My lord! What is it you think you are doing?" she asked, her tone full of reproach.

Merrick hadn't the patience for banter. He wished to know what he wished to know. *Right now.* He gave her no warning of his intentions. He bent to take her mouth in a foraging kiss that made his loins swell with desire.

THE ADVANCE TOOK Chloe completely by surprise.

Lord Lindale's mouth possessed hers, his tongue slipping through the barrier of her lips, tasting with furious abandon. For an instant she could scarcely think to react. Her knees buckled in response and he caught her in his arms, holding her steady for his kiss.

It was fierce and forceful. He took his pleasure as he pleased. But Chloe was not his for the taking! He might have plundered everything else she'd owned, but he wasn't going to take from her the one-and-only thing she had left of value: her reputation. Regaining her senses, she shoved him away.

He went easily, withdrawing, the back of his hand sliding to his mouth, and she thought perhaps he might be disgusted by the kiss. Somehow, it added insult to injury.

But now he appeared to be studying her. "When was the last time I tasted that beautiful mouth?"

For an instant Chloe could only stare, dumbfounded by the question, her mouth hot and bruised from the unexpected advance. She lifted her fingers to ease the sting, her mind numb with the question. It was crude and entirely too personal, not to mention daft, as he'd never dared to kiss her once. And yet, the way he phrased it… the look in his eyes… made her belly quiver and her body respond in ways that confused her as well.

"How… how dare you," she managed, her lips trembling. The bump on his head must have addled his lewd little brain, she decided. "No man has ever dared treat me so basely!"

He had the audacity to smile at that.

"My lord, I was employed to nurse your mother!" she reminded him. "Not to be abused by her intemperate son." His lips curved into a slow smile that infuriated her. "If you ever do that again—"

"Are you threatening me, flower?"

She felt her face flame. "Don't you ever call me that again!" She knew her tone was out of line, but, for once, he must be held accountable!

"Or you'll do what?"

"I will call you out!" she said, and meant it. "I truly will!" she added, when he gave her a dubious look. And having said it, she turned and marched from the room, hurrying away while she still had a coherent thought left in her head.

Zounds! She had always known he was a cad, but his advance was hardly what she had expected. Perhaps he was far more dangerous than she'd perceived?

It was certainly time to rethink her presence here.

CHAPTER 5

*I*n no way would Merrick have normally dared such an advance, but he'd truly believed she must be his wife. That was no excuse, perhaps, but there was no denying it; her reaction to his kiss pleased him immensely. The realization that his brother had never kissed her filled him with no small measure of relief. In fact, it was evident that no man before him had ever touched those soft, sweet, sensuous lips. That knowledge filled him with primal satisfaction.

He smiled to himself over the way she'd clung to him while he'd explored the delicious depths of her mouth. He could still feel every curve of her body pressing against his own, still taste the sweetness of her lips.

She'd threatened to call him out. The very idea turned his smile into a grin. Damn, but she was a fiery vixen. There wasn't a woman in all of Meridian—or London, for that matter—who intrigued him more. His grin widened as he thought of Ian in London. He'd like to see how his brother was faring in his shoes amidst the hordes of eager debutantes. Unless Ian revealed himself at once, he was bound to be immediately inundated by the wearisome social schedule Merrick had managed, by the skin of his teeth, to escape.

But some things could not be avoided.

He made his way into the garden, his gut churning over the thought of facing his birth mother. He would need to reveal himself soon; better that it should be on his own terms.

Would she suspect?

Would she recognize him?

Or, like everyone else he'd met, would she be blind to their differences?

THE GARDEN WAS Fiona's sanctuary.

No one could possibly comprehend what this place meant to her. It reminded her of things that were impossible to forget.

The roses she'd planted were the same ones as those that once crept outside her bedroom window in Meridian. Only here they barely bloomed, despite that she lovingly coaxed them. When, by chance, a blossom emerged, she cherished its rare crimson beauty.

Along the garden pathways, in stark contrast to the deep green rose vines, grew primrose, gayfeather and bright-colored lilies.

At times, such as this morning, whilst she'd looked over Ian as he'd slept, she felt acutely the pain of her loss. And yet... she could not quite regret the past entirely, for Ian had grown into such a remarkable man. And Merrick... she knew he would want for naught. Julian would give him all his heart's desires. Still, so many questions plagued her.

Julian, she knew, would never allow her to risk Merrick's succession to Meridian's throne. He'd threatened her quite implicitly throughout the years, warning her to keep her distance.

But, in truth, he'd never quite released her from his prison, only widened the perimeter of her cell.

Truly, Edward was nothing more than her turnkey. After all, Julian was a selfish, conniving, lying, controlling devil of a man who did not want her, but neither did he wish for anyone else to have her. He'd stolen her life, her child and her freedom. Not for one instant had she had the least control over Glen Abbey Manor. After her father's death, Julian retained the property "for her own good and that of his son's."

And yet the years had not been merciful enough to erase the memory of his affections or the pleasures of his touch. After all this time, those memories could still ravage her heart.

By God, whoever said love and hate were opposites knew not of what they spoke. Fiona loved Julian and despised him at the same time. What she truly wished was that she could simply cease to care.

Noting a particularly healthy section of rose vine, she reached out to better examine what looked to be the promise of a bud. The sight of it gave her heart a little leap of joy. She reached for it, but the bud eluded her, and she eyed the chair with no small measure of disgust. The contraption might be a godsend to those who required it, but for Fiona it was a sentence—another reminder of all her many deceptions—one more horrid lie atop all the rest.

Casting a glance about to make certain no one was watching, she lifted herself ever so slightly from the chair to snatch at the bud.

"HELLO, MOTHER."

The stem pricked her finger, drawing blood. Startled, Fiona gasped. "Ian!" she exclaimed.

Whatever it was that Merrick had come to say, the words stuck in his throat.

She looked so much like the portrait his father had secreted away in his drawer—a little frailer, perhaps, a few more lines on her face, but nevertheless the same.

Her cheeks were tinted red. "What are you doing out of bed—you must rest!"

He longed to ask her what she was doing in that bloody chair if, in fact, she could walk, but he feared his voice would betray him. "I am fine," he said.

She gave him a dubious look. "You always did think yourself invincible. How long have you been standing there?" she asked, averting her gaze as she examined the prick of blood on her finger.

Long enough to see what she obviously hadn't wished for him to see. "Only a moment."

"I see," she said, and pointed to the bench. "Come. Sit a spell and talk with me."

Merrick did as she bade him, uncertain what to say or how to proceed. He sat silently on the bench beside her, regarding his mother for the first time in his life.

It seemed she had her own speech prepared. "I was desperately afraid you would leave me," she said, her voice soft, breaking. Tears clouded her clear blue eyes.

Merrick couldn't feel compassion. In truth, she'd left him long ago. He clenched his jaw, refusing even a sliver of emotion to enter his heart.

"I feared I would never be able to apologize to you for our disagreement last night," she continued. "I do hope you'll understand, Ian, why I cannot give you access to those accounts."

Accounts?

She had refused Ian access to the accounts? His gaze narrowed. "Explain... again," he demanded.

53

She shifted her gaze once more, staring at the tiny prick on the pad of her thumb, blinking away tears. "I cannot," she said, and turned her pale blue gaze upon him. "And, what's more, I must ask you to please leave Edward be. Do not question him further."

"Edward." Merrick repeated the name, making a mental note. His first task, he determined, was to discover who was Edward and what information he wasn't supposed to try to glean from the man.

"Someday... after I am gone, you may pursue this matter to your heart's content, but until that day, you must promise to respect my decision." Her tone was firmer now, and she turned her self-composed gaze upon him.

It was obvious the woman had a caring heart. He didn't sense anything cold or calculating in her gaze, but, clearly, her secrets didn't end with Merrick.

So, why was she in that chair? And what was it she didn't wish her son to discover? And why, in God's good heaven, had she abandoned her child? He had so many questions; none came readily to his lips.

Mulling the situation over, he realized that if he revealed himself now, it would deprive him of the opportunity to know her as his brother knew her. Moreover, if he came forward, he would be forced to reveal Ian's criminal secret, as well. Still, he didn't know how long he could keep up the charade. He might look like his brother, but he wasn't Ian. And his own world was miles apart from this one. There was nothing about this place or this life that was familiar to hm.

"Ahem," came a voice behind him. Merrick turned, following Fiona's gaze.

His mother's brow arched... a perfect imitation of his own mannerism, but no, not an imitation, because they had never before met. The affectation was somehow innate. "Yes, Edward?" she said tersely, addressing the man who stood behind Merrick.

At least he didn't need to go far to answer the first of his questions. Merrick studied Edward. Dressed in servant's livery, there was an air about him that didn't quite fit his station. Edward gave Merrick an accusatory glance and announced, "Miss Simon seems to be taking her leave."

His mother's voice was full of concern. "What do you mean, taking her leave?"

Merrick knew instinctively who they were speaking of. Simon must be her surname.

Edward gave Merrick a pointed glance. "She claims she cannot remain another moment under the same roof as Lord Lindale. She is quite sorry, madame, but feels she must seek new employment."

"Oh, Ian!" Fiona exclaimed, turning her attention toward Merrick. "What have you done now?" She shook her head with unreserved despair.

Merrick lifted a brow, wondering: What else had Ian done to Miss Simon?

"Why must you bait her incessantly?" his mother rebuked. "If you do not like Chloe, simply ignore her!"

So, his mystery woman had a name: *Chloe*. Chloe Simon. How the devil could Ian not like Chloe? It seemed to Merrick that he and his brother had much in common, but this inclination was not one of them. Not only did he like Chloe...he wanted Chloe.

"Good lord! I must insist you speak to her at once," his mother said. "I cannot manage here without her!" She sounded on the verge of hysteria.

Merrick was quite unaccustomed to demands. He'd never heard them from his father, certainly, he didn't anticipate them from the woman seated before him. There were so many questions left unanswered. He wanted—needed—to know more, but the truth was that he didn't want Miss Simon to leave any more than his mother apparently did.

Sighing without the least bit of feigned annoyance, he stood and faced Edward.

There was an unmistakable note of smugness in the man's expression. What had his mother said? That he must not pursue inquiries with Edward? What answers had his brother been seeking from Edward to no avail?

He met Edward's gaze squarely and held it, warning the man without words to stay clear of him.

"Don't worry, Mother." The word sounded awkward upon his lips. "I'll go speak to her," he said, his eyes still fixed upon the steward as he walked away.

"For the love of God, Ian," his mother called after him. "Whatever you do, don't make matters worse!"

CHAPTER 6

*T*he instant the carriage was brought about, Chloe intended to be rid of this infernal place once and for all. In desperation, she'd accepted this position, hoping to recover the deed to their home, but that seemed an impossible task under Edward's endless scrutiny. At any rate, they probably burned the evidence long ago. In light of this fact, she certainly didn't have to suffer the advances of a man she thoroughly loathed, nor was she about to allow her growing affection for Lady Fiona to keep her shackled to this house. Surely, Lady Fiona would find someone else to attend her. And she... well, she would make do.

Chloe's father had been a noteworthy physician, trusted and adored. He'd delivered nearly every bairn born in Glen Abbey during the past thirty years. She was quite certain the townsfolk would continue to seek her services. Her only dilemma was that very few could afford to pay her, and she hadn't any residence from which to conduct her business.

For that matter, she hadn't the first notion where to go.

A knock sounded at her door.

Chloe turned to find Lord Lindale, once again, standing between her and freedom.

She gave him her most disapproving glare and snapped, "What do you want?"

But she really couldn't care less what he wanted; she'd already made up her mind.

For once, Lord Lindale seemed to be weighing his damnable words. "I'm told you plan to leave."

"That is correct." Chloe tugged on her remaining glove, determined not to allow the man to provoke her. She turned again to peer out the window, watching for the carriage to arrive.

"Where is it you intend to go?" he asked as though he believed she had no available options.

But, of course, she didn't. That, however, was not his concern. Chloe spun to face him, furious that he should be so crude as to point out the impracticality of her decision. "Where I go is absolutely none of your affair, my lord."

He stepped into the room then, and Chloe instinctively retreated, hating herself for showing any weakness. Instinctively, she lifted two fingers to her lips. Even still… they felt… thoroughly kissed.

He averted his gaze, peering down at his boots, placing his hands behind his back—an oddly docile gesture for him. And now he seemed to be contemplating his words—hardly usual for a man who was never at a loss for sarcasm or wit.

At last, his gaze met hers. "Would it change your mind if I apologized?"

Apologized?

Chloe arched a brow. It certainly wasn't like him to offer apologies for anything—not ever—but it was too late for apologies. "No," she replied. "But, no matter, it would certainly be the gentlemanly thing to do."

He arched a brow. "I take it you think I need lessons in social intercourse?"

Chloe lifted her chin. "My lord... one need not be noble born to know that no gentleman would ever treat a woman so rudely."

"Alas," he said. "It wasn't the gentleman in me responding to you, I fear. I beg forgiveness, Chloe..."

He took another step into the room and Chloe sucked in a breath but stood her ground. She glanced over her shoulder. It wasn't as though she had any choice but to stand firm; there wasn't anywhere left to retreat to. He took yet another step toward her and her heart beat quickened.

"As for my desire... I have known wives who did not think it so crude to be desired by their husbands."

Chloe tried in vain to eradicate the memory of his kiss. "Perhaps, my lord, but I am neither a wife, nor a husband," she said tartly.

At her declaration, he came no further. He stood midway, putting his hands back in a non-confrontational stance, and Chloe released the breath she'd not realized she'd held.

His voice softened and his eyes slitted as they regarded her. "You would hardly be mistaken for a husband," he said, and the silky sound of his voice sent a shiver down her spine.

Why did he seem so different? And why did her legs suddenly feel as unsubstantial as pudding?

Chloe fidgeted under the heat of his scrutiny. "Really, my lord, this is hardly an appropriate conversation."

"You must forgive me, Chloe," he said, and the intimate way he spoke her name made Chloe's breath catch. "I am afraid I was beset by my injuries and did not realize what it was I was doing."

Chloe arched a brow over his explanation. It was true that he hadn't been himself since his fall.

He gave her a disarming smile—one she'd never witnessed firsthand, though she knew he employed it all too often. She'd watched him work his wiles on unsuspecting women and had sworn to never be his victim. And yet... that smile... it made her heart beat a little faster, confusing her.

IT WAS all Merrick could do not to claim her into his arms and carry her away, like some crude barbarian. He might regret his approach, but hardly the kiss.

In fact, he wanted to kiss her again. *This very moment.*

Somehow, he restrained himself. One step nearer and he would lose his reason. The delicate scent of roses teased him even at this distance. It made him want to bury his face against her throat and inhale the sweet scent of her skin.

She looked so beautifully indignant. And lord-a-mercy, by the way she had touched her lips, he knew that the woman in her had reveled in his passion.

Unbidden, a vision came to him of her straddling him, her rich, auburn hair spilling like silk down the length of her back, her delicate face in the throes of passion, and his loins tightened.

God help him, he could still taste her upon his lips...

She hitched her chin. "Arrive at your point, my lord. What is it you want?"

What he wanted, was her. What he needed was her help, he decided. Merrick needed an ally. "I'm afraid the fall must have, indeed, addled my brain, Chloe. Clearly, I have been a wretch and today I see the error of my ways."

The arch of her brow lifted higher. "I could have told you that, my lord."

Saucy vixen. "Alas, I am mortified to say I had forgotten who you were. In fact, I thought you must be my wife. Isn't that amusing?" he asked.

Her brow furrowed. "Quite," she agreed, but she didn't return his smile.

"I assure you it will never happen again," he said, knowing it was a lie. If the opportunity arose, he would surely seize it. Kissing Chloe Simon was suddenly at the very top of his list of wants. However, at the moment, he wanted her compliance and he wasn't ashamed to admit that he would say anything to obtain it. He wanted—needed—her presence at Glen Abbey Manor whilst he continued his quest. "As compensation, I will give you an increase in wages," he added. "That is... if you agree to remain."

She gave him a skeptical glance. "You did not know who I was?"

He shook his head. "Truly." That much wasn't a lie. Neither was the pain that flared suddenly in his head, and he lifted a hand defensively to his forehead. It ached him like the devil.

For her part, Chloe seemed to be pondering his explanation and he closed his eyes, suddenly dizzy, lifting a hand to his temple as he stumbled.

Chloe rushed forward. "Oh! You shouldn't be out of bed. Come," she demanded, pulling him firmly toward the bed. "Sit!" she said, and Merrick did as she bade him. Tilting her head this way and that, she studied him as he sat, inspecting his injured head.

"Look at me. Can you see me clearly?" she asked. He did, and blinked at the look of concern nestled in her beautiful dark eyes. He couldn't at once respond, so entranced was he by the unfathomable warm depths of her gaze.

"My lord?"

Merrick shook himself free of his momentary stupor to find Chloe regarding him very critically. She reached out to examine his wound, nibbling gently at her already swollen lip. Her voice when she spoke was sober. "I've heard of memory lapses arising after severe injuries to the head. Tell me, is there aught else you do not recall?"

It wasn't precisely a lie. "It's coming back to me slowly, Chloe. But I don't remember much at all."

DEVIL TAKE HIM. Chloe believed him. He'd never once before called her by her given name—always Miss Simon. But she was certain this was only a temporary loss of memory. As the injury healed, the fog would lift from his brain, and then he would doubtless return to his obnoxious self.

"I don't wish to alarm my mother," he said.

Chloe didn't either, but she wasn't going to allow him to walk away with impunity. "An increase in wages, you say?" Additional funds might allow her to open her own clinic someday. If she could save enough, she would be able to continue to look after the sick and the poor. She lifted her chin, determined to ask for far more than she knew he was prepared to give. Miser that he was, he would surely try to bargain her down. "Well, then... perhaps I might be persuaded if you would consider *doubling* my salary."

There was no bartering, not a bit. "Consider it done," he said to Chloe's surprise.

Chloe's brows lifted. "Are you quite certain, my lord?" The fall had, indeed, juggled his brain!

"It appears you are indispensable," he said for answer. "To my mother... and... to me. Thank you."

Chloe's breath caught at his look. His clear blue eyes

seemed to say far more than his words. "N-not at all," she stammered. "But I'm certain for that fee Lady Fiona could hire someone more experienced to nurse her."

His blue eyes were fixed upon her, entrapping her gaze. "It is not my mother who needs you most," he said softly, and he rose from the bed. Chloe's heart quickened a beat, but she couldn't seem to look away.

Something strange passed between them in that instant, some connection she couldn't decipher. "You... you should rest, my lord," she said breathlessly.

"I'll see the funds are available to be dispensed at once." His gaze released her at long last and he turned to go. Stepping over her baggage at the door, he paused before taking his leave, smiling wistfully. "You would make a lovely wife," he said.

And then he was gone.

Chloe stood, flabbergasted. She hadn't the first inkling what had transpired. Indeed, Lord Lindale didn't seem at all himself.

Could it be he was telling the truth?

It was quite rare to lose one's memory entirely, but not unheard of. If it were true, perhaps she could use his present state to her advantage? And perhaps the deed to her home wasn't lost, after all?

He'd said she was indispensable.

It's not my mother who needs you most, he'd said, and the memory of his words made her shiver, though she didn't trust him. He wanted something from her; Chloe was certain of it. She'd never known Ian to flatter anyone without cause. There was a time she'd believed him charming, but she'd very quickly come to realize that every word that came out of his mouth was coldly calculated. He'd grown from a boy who'd defied his station to play with commoners into a coldhearted, greedy landlord who took food from the mouths of babes, and who cared only for his own pleasures. It would behoove her to tread lightly with Lindale, and to believe none of his words.

"WHAT DO YOU MEAN, the funds are not available?" Merrick asked, stunned by the disclosure. He sat in a chair facing the steward's desk and took in the state of the room.

It was comfortably furnished and slightly less kept than the rest of the household. A film of dust covered the draperies and furnishings… everywhere but the desk, which was apparently well used. But, unlike the rest of the house, it was obvious this office was not maintained daily by the servants.

"Precisely that, my lord. The funds are not available to you."

The cocky bastard had informed him very baldly that he had no right to peruse the books. They were under lock and key, he'd declared—a lock to which, apparently, he had the only key.

Why would a steward have sole possession of the estate books and house keys?

Was it possible the estate belonged, not to Ian, but to his mother? If so, how was it that Fiona trusted Edward over her own son?

Merrick rephrased his question. "By not available *to me*, do you mean they do not exist? Or do you mean that I cannot personally access them?"

Edward stood rigidly by the cabinets where the ledgers were all kept, obstinately shaking his head. "As I've said previously, my lord, I am not at liberty to speak of household investments. If you wish to know more, you must broach the matter with Lady Fiona."

"I see," Merrick said, and then added, surmising, "So

you would send me to my mother, and she returns me to you, and it goes precisely nowhere?"

The steward averted his gaze. "I am sorry, my lord."

Like hell he was. It was perfectly clear by the man's smug expression that he wouldn't be persuaded to reveal anything more. But Merrick fully intended to get to the heart of the matter. He wasn't accustomed to being refused; it didn't set well with him at all. Imagine telling the Prince of Meridian he couldn't have what he so pleased. "I suggest you find a way to obtain those funds," he told the steward, eyeing him pointedly. "Miss Simon will be paid as agreed upon, and I have no doubt my mother will tell you the same."

The steward's arrogant facade cracked just a bit. "Yes, my lord, she is, indeed, quite fond of Miss Simon, but—"

Merrick stood abruptly and made to leave without excusing himself. "Just do it, Edward," he snapped, and he left before his temper could no longer be restrained.

At least he now understood what answers his brother had sought from Edward to no avail. He experienced a momentary pang of regret for Ian. Was this what drove his brother to thievery?

It didn't matter.

Thievery was hardly a noble pursuit—no matter that Chloe seemed to think it was.

But as far as Edward was concerned, the steward only thought he was in control. Merrick was about to set the man on his heels. However, his first task was to find out to whom the estate belonged—to his father or to Fiona. Merrick suspected the miser was his father, in which case, Edward had better find himself a rock to crawl beneath. He would make a mash of him, to be sure. But, at the instant his greatest dilemma was in getting a message to Ryo without alerting Ian, his father or his mother. Ryo was the one-and-only person Merrick felt he could rely upon without question. Despite that the old man's loyalties lay primarily with Merrick's father, ultimately Ryo would do what his conscience dictated.

Intuitively, Merrick had a feeling Ian wouldn't reveal himself straightaway, so there must be some way Merrick could alert Ryo that he had the wrong brother... or, at the very least, plant a seed.

CHAPTER 7

*T*he house was dark as a sin. The office itself was gloomier. Although it was impossible to make out anything without a lamp, Chloe didn't dare light one and call attention to herself snooping at this late hour.

During the time she'd been in residence at Glen Abbey, she'd never dared enter the steward's office. Late in the afternoon following her threatened resignation, she was afforded the perfect opportunity. Edward left in a huff and he had yet to return. Lord Lindale, too, ventured out for the evening—where he'd gone nobody knew, but they were both likely to return soon. Alas, she hadn't been able to slip away until Lady Fiona fell asleep and the servants—few that remained— all retired to their quarters.

Knowing she had precious little time, she hurriedly sifted through papers, bringing one pile, then another, to the window to read them by the moonlight shining in through the sliver in the draperies.

Thus far, it was all a worthless jumble—receipts for payments made and purchase orders for the kitchen. She'd already tried the cabinets to no avail. They were sealed tighter than a beggar's grip about a copper.

A single piece of paper secured beneath a squatting silver elephant caught her attention and she plucked it out from under the paperweight and took it to the window.

"Notice of eviction," she read, scanning the page for a name. "Rusty Broun... for lack of rents paid."

Shock stole her breath. Her eyes narrowed with disgust. Rusty had only just lost his youngest daughter. The callousness over it all made her furious. She wanted to tear the document to shreds and to toss it into Lindale's face.

"Find something interesting?" a voice said at her back.

Chloe's heart nearly leaped out of her breast. She spun to find the very devil peering at her from across the room.

His face cast in shadows, he'd never looked so menacing. Good grief, she never even heard him enter. He strode forward with purpose and Chloe gasped in fright.

Where now was her mettle? She berated herself.

But, to her dismay, he'd never looked more beautifully dangerous—Lucifer himself looming out of the darkness.

He closed the distance between them in just a few strides and snatched the document from her hand. He peered at it an instant, his face registering no emotion. Then he looked back at her and asked pointedly, "What are you doing here?"

"I was..." Chloe fumbled for an explanation. "I mean to say... Well, I went to put out the lamp in your mother's room..."

His brow arched higher. "Her room is in the east wing," he reminded her.

Chloe nipped her lower lip, feeling utterly trapped. Zounds, she was a terrible liar. "Yes, well... when I was in the hall, you see... I spied someone stealing toward the steward's office...so I followed."

She tried not to roll her eyes over the stupid explanation, but it was evident he didn't believe her. His eyes clearly registered doubt. "Is that so?"

Chloe nodded.

His face remained an impenetrable mask as he peered down once more at the document in his hand, then proceeded to fold it whilst he studied her in turn. He slipped the document into his coat pocket.

Chloe held her tongue under his painful scrutiny. God have mercy, she wanted to say so much, but something about the look in his eyes kept her silenced.

"You're a lovely little liar," he said. "What is it you were searching for, Chloe?"

The pang in her heart stilled her tongue. She was so close to uncovering the truth now, she could feel it. But if he realized she suspected him of stealing the deed, he would send her packing. "I..." She averted her gaze, unable to look him in the eyes, but she managed an easy tone. "Nothing... truly, my lord."

He opened his mouth to speak, but closed it again, his attention diverted by the echo of footfalls approaching down the hall. Chloe half expected him to drag her out to face the constable; instead he seized her by the arm and quickly pulled her behind the heavy draperies. He placed a hand firmly against her mouth, shushing her, and Chloe was utterly confused by his reaction.

The curtains were still swaying when the door came open. Lord Lindale's hand lingered over her mouth, but he drew it slightly away, scarce touching her lips. The heat emanating from his skin stilled not only her tongue but her breath and heart as well.

It was Edward who'd nearly stumbled upon them; she could tell by the prudish gait of his footsteps. He lit a lamp at the desk and sat down, Chloe assumed. She heard the chair scrape backward and then the sound of a drawer opening. Next, she heard the scrape of a pen. Thankfully, he hadn't noticed their presence. She prayed the curtain would still completely, lest they be discovered—but why Lord Lindale should fear discovery, Chloe hadn't the first inkling.

Something wasn't right....

STILL CONTEMPLATING the document in his pocket, Merrick listened while Edward fiddled about in the room.

It didn't make sense; if Ian and Rusty were bedfellows, why would his brother oust the man from his home? He remembered the chap's admiration and devotion and felt gobsmacked by the notion.

His gut told him that Ian hadn't the first clue... or, if he did, he hadn't any control over the situation... which only validated his suspicions that their father retained control of this estate.

But he couldn't think now...

He drew Chloe gently against him, knowing full well that she wouldn't dare reveal them. Her back pressing against him, the gentle curves of her body teased him. The scent of her intoxicated him, muddling his thoughts. It was all he could do not to sweep aside the curls of her hair to brush his lips against the soft curve of her nape. Jesus wept, he didn't want to scare her into bolting, or he'd have done precisely that.

It was torment—to be so near her and yet so far. His loins reacted at once, hardening.

What could she have been searching for?

At the desk, he heard the sound of a pen scratching over paper and then the jingling of keys. A cabinet opened, then closed. And then, again, the jingling of

SEDUCED BY A PRINCE

keys as the cabinet was locked once more. The lamp went out and the door closed.

They were alone again.

"Shhhh," he said. "He might not yet be gone."

"Why did you not reveal me?" Chloe asked, sounding breathless.

Merrick was having trouble getting air into his lungs, as well. "I had my reasons."

She pressed him. "I don't understand. Why should it concern you if Edward were to discover you here? This is your home."

Merrick suspected otherwise. Who did the steward report to? How much autonomy did he have? He wanted a look at those ledgers.

"Tell me, my lord," she persisted. "*Why* would *you* hide?"

"Because..." Merrick inhaled the scent of her sweet skin and tried not to lose track of his thoughts. He gave her as much truth as he dared. "I believe Edward is embezzling. I am looking for proof. And you, Miss Simon..." He brushed a finger along the soft underside of her chin, almost caressing. "What are you really doing here?"

"I told you..." Her impertinence returned and she shrugged free of him. "You can release me now, my lord. We are quite alone!"

Merrick did as she asked and smiled tightly as she boxed her way out of the draperies. He followed her out.

Facing him now as he emerged, her shoulders squared, her chin tipped defiantly. He could barely see her face in the shadows, but it was impossible to miss the challenge in her glittering eyes. "If you do not believe me, I can still tender my resignation."

It was a bluff, Merrick knew, but one he wasn't about to call. The last thing he wished was to see her go. He needed her. "That won't be necessary," he assured.

"Very well, then. If that will be all, my lord, I believe I shall retire, at last."

He couldn't help but grin at her fortitude. Never in his life had anyone dared speak to him so cheekily. "Don't trip over any intruders on the way," he taunted.

But she'd already turned to go before the last words were out of his mouth. "Do not fret, my lord. Next time, I shall be certain to hand over the keys to the silver, as well!"

FIONA CONTEMPLATED Edward's disappearance the prior evening. "The color in your legs is good today," Chloe said, interrupting her reverie.

She gave Fiona a questioning glance—or at least, it seemed to be a question. At times Fiona was certain Chloe must realize she was lying. She averted her gaze and Chloe returned to the task of massaging her legs.

Guilt gnawed at her.

Every day the lies grew in weight. This morning the burden was entirely unbearable. One lie conceived another and yet another. Of late, she could scarcely even look at her own son, for all the deception.

What sort of mother did that make her?

She was utterly torn.

Indeed, she had the power to change their circumstances, but if she told Ian the truth, she risked losing her son. And there was no guarantee Julian would give him the same treatment he'd given Merrick. After all these years, she didn't know Julian anymore, and his father was bound to dismiss him entirely.

Nor, in truth, did she wish to risk Merrick's inheritance. She knew Julian had gone to great lengths to en-sure his bloodline was never questioned. But, for the first time Fiona paused to consider the woman Julian had wed in her place. In all these years, she hadn't dared, because anger had been her ally. God forgive her, but she hadn't wished to like or feel sorry for Julian's wife. And yet, what must it feel like to have someone else's child foisted upon you? To know he would inherit over your own blood? *Did it make her bitter? Sad?*

Fiona knew Julian's wife never conceived. Had he married her in name only, keeping her at length? Or was it she who rebuffed Julian?

Truly, she didn't wish to say he deserved it. No matter how much Julian had hurt her, no one deserved to suffer their entire lives. She only prayed Merrick had not suffered the wrath of a scorned wife.

Sighing deeply, Fiona stared at the hands so gently working her legs till they blurred through the mist in her tears.

Chloe, too, seemed lost in her own reverie. This morning, Fiona was heartily grateful for the silence.

But, once again, she considered the young woman standing before her. Chloe wasn't a member of the *haute ton* by any means, but if her son could chance to win her heart, it would remain true to him forever-more. That was all Fiona's father had ever truly wished for her—a good man to cherish her. That's what she wanted for her son.

Having lived on both sides of the proverbial fence, she understood the value of love versus money. In the end, money didn't keep one warm at night, nor did a title put food upon one's table.

Yes, it was true. Once upon a time, she had dreamt of wedding a prince and living in splendor. Now she realized that too often values were misplaced for the love of money. From the day Ian came into the world, she'd wanted nothing more than for him to be happy.

And he'd been such a contented babe.

As a boy, he'd lost some of his joie de vivre.

As a man, he was hardly ever content.

Her son was, unfortunately, somewhat of a crusader. He seemed to feel it his lot in life to better the lives of others. That in itself wasn't particularly troubling; it was more the way he chose to go about it. His secret life was a mother's nightmare.

She knew precisely what he was up to—and he knew she knew it, as well, but there was little she could do about it. She'd already tried and failed.

What had begun as a simple fib to draw him out and to ease her suspicions had become a horrible sentence. Not only were her worst fears confirmed, her lies further imprisoned her. And worse, sitting in that devilish contraption all day long was making her an invalid in truth. Some days, she could barely feel any sensation in her legs.

Thank the Lord for Chloe!

"I have been thinking," Chloe announced as she continued to massage her limbs.

"Yes, dear?"

"There is a treatment I read about in last year's published lectures—quite experimental, but perhaps it might be worth a thought."

"What is it?"

"Vital air."

Fiona furrowed her brow. "Vital air?"

"Yes, my lady."

"Fiona," she said, and Chloe smiled timidly.

Undeterred, she continued, "There was this man, you see. He was apparently quite weak. As a matter of treatment, his physician put him on a course of vital air. During the time he respired it, he felt a comfortable heat, which distributed itself throughout all his limbs. In mere weeks, his strength increased, and he was able to take short walks. However, this man was in the last stages of consumption, though I must wonder. You see, vital air is nothing more than pure oxygen gas. When exposed to it, plants develop at an increased rate of growth. It would make sense that it somehow promotes growth of healthy tissue within the body, as well—much the same way increased blood flow will do. That's what I'm doing now with this massage. Alas, I cannot say it is a certain cure. I'm at an end as to how to treat you, my lady."

"Fiona," she said again.

Chloe's expression was full of apology. "Try as I have, I've not been able to find and remedy the cause of your…"

"Lameness," Fiona finished for her. "You may call it what it is, Chloe. Never mince words with me. Tell me, is this treatment terribly exorbitant? Does it hurt?"

"I would have to look into the cost. But it shouldn't hurt at all. In fact, they say it produces a sensation of agreeable warmth about the region of the chest along with a comfortable sensation throughout the body."

Fiona sighed. "Very well. Let us consider it, then," she said. "You're a godsend, Chloe."

Chloe averted her gaze. "In truth, you might do better to hire yourself a proper physician," she suggested.

"Rubbish! I already have a proper physician!" Fiona replied without pause. "And she happens to be quite accomplished. Never suggest such a thing again!"

Fiona understood Chloe must feel inadequate after the loss of Rusty Broun's child. But Fiona had never met a woman, nor a man, who tried as hard as Chloe. She sighed heavily, wearied as she watched Chloe work in vain.

Poor Chloe, didn't she realize; there hadn't been an accident at all? Fiona had taken the carriage out alone with a devilish design. Knowing Ian would follow, she'd run her own carriage off the road and then lain in wait for her son to come along. Like a silly fool, she'd claimed that Hawk had driven her off the road and then tried to rob her—to which Ian was supposed to have confessed that such an incident was quite impossible, because, of course, he was Hawk.

But he hadn't done any sort of thing.

Instead the wily boy insisted they report the robbery to the constable, and he'd called in the physician to examine Fiona at once. Chloe's father, of course.

Unfortunately, Fiona hadn't learned her lesson and her deceptions had only begun. Once her lies began, pride was her downfall. Like a dolt, she'd talked Chloe's father into covering for her. Alas, Fiona might be able to fool Chloe for a time, but her father had been far too seasoned.

But then... everything went from bad to worse.

To everyone's utter shock, Chloe's father's heart failed him, and Fiona felt responsible for his death—her plotting had most certainly caused him undue stress. And knowing that, without the deed to their land, Chloe wouldn't be able to remain in their home, Fiona had offered Chloe a position as her nurse. So here she was, eight months later, still sitting in an invalid chair while her son was still risking his life and limb to change the circumstances of others—all because of Fiona's lies.

But there must be something she could do—if nothing else, at least for Chloe and Ian. While Chloe worked on her legs, Fiona worked on the problem.

76

ALONE IN THE LIBRARY, Merrick retrieved the eviction notice from his coat pocket and sat in a chair, contemplating his mother's involvement.

How much did Fiona know of Edward's actions?

His gut told him that Ian was as much in the dark as was Merrick. But what of his mother?

Setting his feet atop a stool, he stared at the incriminating document, unable to shake a growing feeling of unease.

The constable called yet again this morn, questioning Merrick about the missing vehicle. Merrick had assured the man that he hadn't the least notion of what he was speaking, but it hadn't seemed to assuage the man. No wonder Ian fled with his coach; in the short time Merrick had been literally wearing his shoes, Ian's life had begun to feel like a chessboard with the king in check.

What he needed right now was to speak with Rusty Broun, only he didn't know where to reach him.

But Chloe would know.

He smiled at the thought of her.

Saucy wench.

And suddenly he couldn't wait to see her.

Folding the document, he replaced it within his coat pocket and went to find the delightful but obstinate tenant of his thoughts.

CHAPTER 8

"Why should you require my assistance?" Chloe asked, incensed that Lord Lindale would involve her in his odious task. "You know very well where everyone in this town lives, my lord. If they don't pay rents, your agents go knocking."

"Because I don't remember," Lord Lindale replied.

"Oh, but you'll remember soon enough, I'm certain," Chloe said, and continued toward the garden to collect Lady Fiona.

How dare he ask her to accompany him to deliver Rusty's eviction notice! Or, at least, she assumed that was why he was bound there. What other business would Lord Lindale have with that poor man?

"I'm afraid it cannot wait for my memory to return. I need to speak with him today."

Chloe spun to face him abruptly, her temper rekindling. "Are you so greedy you cannot allow that man time to grieve before ousting him from his home? What sort of monster are you, my lord?"

He seemed, for an instant, without answer to her question, and then he said, "That is not why I wish to see him."

"Why then?"

He couldn't seem to answer.

Chloe lifted both brows. "Forgive me if I do not believe you, Lord Lindale, but I can certainly read, and I know what I saw last night."

"Dammit, woman, has anyone ever told you you're an impudent wench?"

Chloe inhaled sharply, offended by his rude question. "Well, of course not!"

"Well, you are."

"And you are greedy, selfish, repugnant, spoiled—"

Chloe gasped in surprise when he took her into his arms suddenly, drawing her against him so tightly that she could barely breathe—not that she could have anyway with his mouth so near to her own.

The look in his eyes was unlike anything she'd ever experienced; hungry in a way no food or drink could satiate.

Her heart slammed against her ribs as he lowered his head, so his mouth was mere inches from her own. God help her, his lips were wickedly tempting. She couldn't help but remember the taste of him and suddenly crave him; the memory would never be eradicated from her mind, not so long as she lived.

Her voice sounded small even to her own ears. "You aren't…going to… kiss me… are you?"

MERRICK COULD BARELY RESTRAIN HIMSELF. His tongue craved the taste of her mouth like a drunkard craved whiskey. He longed to savor her entire body… kiss her in places she'd never imagined wanting to be kissed.

He wouldn't lie. "I was thinking about it."

Her breath came in a rush. "You promised!"

"That I did," he acknowledged, his voice hoarse. His lips were suddenly parched. "But I find myself… regretting…"

79

Damn, but she was beautiful, with those deep, dark eyes...

She gazed at him almost expectantly and he couldn't decide whether she was afraid of his answer or eager for receive his kiss. "Regretting?"

"That you aren't my wife," he said low. "If you were, I'd kiss the impudence straight from those lovely lips."

CHLOE FELT SUDDENLY dizzied by his words. She should, by all accounts, be incensed, but his declaration left her feeling... strangely bereft. Surely she didn't long for his kiss?

Lord Lindale was in every way Hawk's diametrical opposite. How could she want this man in her life?

"It is broad daylight, my lord," she reminded him, putting her hands against his chest to shove him away. His skin was firm beneath her touch. "You may not give a care about your actions, but I beg you only consider my reputation. Release me at once!"

He grinned a devastating grin—one that nearly disarmed her. "If you will promise to accompany me, I shall do anything you wish."

Chloe arched a brow. "Anything?"

He nodded, still grinning. In fact, his smile widened. Chloe was certain it hadn't escaped him that she was, inadvertently, exploring his chest, her fingers dancing over his coat. She swallowed convulsively, stilling her wayward fingers, and she prayed that once he let go of her she wouldn't crumple into an embarrassing heap at his feet.

"If I join you, you must destroy Rusty's eviction notice."

"Done!" he said at once, even joyfully, startling her with the emphatic response. He released her suddenly and pulled the document from his coat pocket, then proceeded to rip it into shreds. And he kept tearing it until there was nothing left but tiny pieces, then he scattered them on the lawn.

"Let's go for a ride!" he said ardently, and Chloe wondered what it was she had agreed to. He seemed far too agreeable to have destroyed his very reason for visiting Rusty Broun.

So, then, if he didn't intend to see Rusty in order to evict him, what, then, was his business with the man?

Chloe was still contemplating that very question as they rode together in the coach—Lindale far too gleeful as he sat, peering out the window.

In fact, Chloe suddenly realized how dangerous it was to be in his presence, because he reminded her this instant, not of that greedy, selfish tyrant he was, but a charming young boy on his first outing. He examined things now as though he'd never set eyes upon them before. It was entirely too disturbing.

"What is that?" he asked, pointing to a small cottage they passed along the way.

Chloe grit her teeth. "That," she apprised him, "was the home where I spent my whole life."

He turned to regard her suddenly, his look far too innocent, considering his question. "How quaint," he said, peering at her very curiously. "It's rather close to the manor, is it not?"

Chloe held her tongue. It was all she could do not to fly at him and scratch out his eyes as she remembered the afternoon of her father's funeral. "Yes, it is, my lord."

"Why do you not stay there and simply make the trek each morn to tend my mother?"

Chloe gave him her most cutting glance. "I would if I could, but it is no longer my own."

"Why? Did you sell it?"

Chloe tilted her head, giving him a disbelieving

glance. "Do you truly not remember anything, my lord?"

He seemed to weigh his answer before giving it. "Some things, perhaps, not others."

Chloe peered out from the carriage and watched as the cottage faded behind them, along with her life's dreams and all her happy memories. "I lost possession of that cottage the day after my father's death," she informed him.

"Why?"

"Because I could not produce the deed." She turned and cast him a pointed glance. "The cottage is now *yours*, my lord. Because I could not prove it was a gift—from your grandfather to my father. It reverted to you when I failed to produce evidence."

Lindale's smile faded. He nodded, seeming to realize the insulting nature of his question to her. "I see," he said, and Chloe averted her gaze, peering out the window as the carriage lumbered off the main road, onto another, narrower, bumpier road that led to Rusty's small farm.

They rode in silence, except for the rattling of their teeth as they traveled over the rugged dirt road.

"Was it me who came to evict you?" he inquired after a moment's contemplation. His brows were furrowed.

Chloe couldn't look at him. "Of course not. As always, you sent Edward to do your worst."

"Really," he said, but it didn't appear to be a question at all, and Chloe didn't feel the need to respond.

If he felt badly, then good. He should feel badly. Memory loss, or not, he had done what he had done, and he was who he was. There were no excuses. But she really shouldn't allow herself to be fooled by his new, charming disposition. He was still the same person, she reminded herself, and he'd surely return to his old self again as soon as his memory returned.

There was a long length of weighted silence, during which time he appeared to be considering her disclosure.

"Tell me... why could you not produce the deed?" he asked after what felt like an eternity.

Chloe turned to meet his gaze, wanting to see his reaction. "Because it was *stolen*, my lord." She spat the word with all the contempt she felt over the thievery. And, make no mistake, it was burgled. She knew that beyond a shadow of doubt.

No remorse registered upon his face.

Chloe cursed his memory loss that he couldn't give her any satisfaction. She wanted him to feel horrid over what he'd done. She knew good and well it was him who'd stolen that deed; no one else had anything to profit from its disappearance. "While I was at my father's funeral," she added without blinking, and she willed him to see the hurt he had caused.

This time his brows rose ever-so slightly, registering not the guilt she wanted but something more like... consternation?

"THEY BLAMED IT ON HAWK, but I know with certainty that it wasn't him."

Merrick's mood plummeted.

"Why?" he pressed.

Chloe arched a brow. "Because he wouldn't take from people in need only to give it to the likes of you."

Merrick felt her accusation like a kick to his belly. No wonder she loathed him! If she thought him responsible for the fall of her fortune, there was little wonder she spoke to him at all—much less remained under the same roof.

Unless...

Suddenly, it made sense—her foray into the steward's office, her unwavering animosity toward Ian and her very presence at Glen Abbey Manor. She was hoping to recover the deed to her cottage.

It was a fruitless effort, Merrick could have apprised her. If, in fact, Edward was responsible for the theft, he would have burned that evidence long ago.

That's what Merrick would have done.

They rode the remainder of the way in silence, while Merrick considered the course he should take. Somehow he must prove to Chloe that Ian was not responsible for all her miseries, but before he could do that, he must first determine that to be the case. His gut told him that his brother might, in fact, be a thief, but he hadn't a heart as cold as the one it would take to sweep a girl's home from under her feet.

He also needed to know what involvement his mother had in this. And he needed to discover a way to reverse the decline of this town's welfare. His own family matters, he sensed, were at the heart of all that was foul here.

"We're here," Chloe said, as the carriage stopped before a small stone house.

Having heard their approach, Rusty's wife met them at the door. She gave Chloe a hearty welcome, and then silently thumbed Merrick in the proper direction when he asked about Rusty, though not before giving him a wary glance. Wiping her hands on her apron, she watched from the porch as he made his way through the oat field, looking for her husband, and he heard their whispers the instant he turned his back.

He found Rusty at work with his three young daughters trailing behind him. The youngest appeared to be about four. In her hands, she carried a crude doll. The middle child appeared to be about six. Her fingers were curled possessively about the handle of a small bucket. The oldest was probably about seven. In her hands, she held clumps of weeds, which she tossed into her sister's bucket.

"We're helping, Papa, aren't we?" she said, looking at her father, obviously seeking his praise.

"Yes, lass," Rusty assured. "You're a fine wee helper, ye are."

The youngest of the three noticed Merrick first and startled. She tugged desperately at her father's pant leg. "Papa, papa!" she exclaimed, pointing at Merrick.

Rusty spun to face him, surprise evident in his expression. "Lord Lindale!"

"Who is that, Papa?" his middle daughter inquired.

Instead of ushering his children away or shushing them, the big, burly man swooped down to lift up his youngest into his arms. She squirmed and squealed to be let down. "So ye think you're too old to be held?" Rusty asked her, pretending offense. He plastered a big, puckering kiss on her sweet round cheek, then answered her question. "That, my wee sprite... is Lord Lindale." He gave Merrick a nod. "He's the man kind enough to allow us to rent this fine piece of land."

Merrick felt an inexplicable stab of guilt.

Rusty set his daughter down, patting her upon the head. With big blue eyes, she peered up at Merrick and asked innocently, "Can you make the dirt grow more food? We are hungry and our sister Ana went to heaven, but we don't wanna go to Heaven yet."

Rusty's other daughter shook her head very adamantly, seconding her sister's sentiments. "She din't like to eat anyfing but carrots. But Papa can't only grow carrots." She peered up at her father. "Right, Papa?"

Merrick didn't know what to say to the child.

A glance at Rusty revealed a pale face and eyes that were visibly glazed. He scratched his forehead, trying to make the effort a casual one, and then averted his gaze, but Merrick saw the control he struggled to maintain and turned his attention to the girls to give the man time to compose himself.

He got down on one knee, at their level, and said solemnly, "We'll see what we can do about getting you more carrots."

CHLOE WATCHED FROM THE PORCH, with Emma, Rusty's wife, as Merrick fell to his knees to speak to one of Rusty's daughters. Something about his body language made Chloe smile softly, despite the pall their conversation had cast over her mood.

"What does he want?" Emma Broun asked.

"I haven't the first clue," confessed Chloe. But she dearly hoped it had nothing to do with that document he'd shredded.

Then, again, she hadn't actually inspected the paper —she hoped he hadn't anticipated her request and disposed of something else entirely.

Chloe turned to find Emma studying her. "You like him?"

"Oh, no! I certainly do not!"

Chloe didn't mean to sound so vehement, but she simply couldn't have anyone thinking she had feelings for Lord Lindale. Even if he weren't a cad, he was not for her. He was an earl; she was nothing more than a physician's daughter.

Emma turned her attention toward Lindale, his body language easy and not the least bit unfriendly. "In any case, I think 'e likes you, Miss Chloe."

Chloe shook her head. It was entirely Emma's imagination.

Or was it.

He did seem to like kissing her. She could tell by

the way he was always ogling her mouth. Unbidden, she thought about the kiss they'd shared, and her cheeks warmed. She was heartily glad Emma was no longer looking at her. But, to her dismay, her body responded at once: Her breasts tingled as she watched him speak to the girls and she licked her lips gone suddenly dry.

The taste of him lingered.

Sweet lord, she was afraid Emma might be right. The fall hadn't merely addled his brain, it put strange thoughts into his head. Crossing her arms over her breasts, she vowed to guard her heart.

MERRICK TURNED his attention to the youngest child. "My, that's a fine doll you've got there," he said. "What's her name?"

The little girl threw an arm over her eyes so that she couldn't see him, obviously too embarrassed to reply.

"She doesn't like strangers," the eldest daughter explained, taking her sister's hand protectively. "It used to be called Mairi, but now we call it Ana."

"We painted her hair red," said the middle child, seizing the doll from her little sister. "But it din't look good... see." She held it out for Merrick's inspection, pointing to the doll's bright, red head. The worn-out little doll was made of burlap, with a string tied about a small round rock to simulate the head and neck. There were no arms or legs and the face was also painted, very likely, by their mother, though the hair was clearly, but lovingly, painted by a different hand—one of theirs, or perhaps all of them. The toy certainly had seen better days, and he thought about all the things he'd taken for granted as a child... all the toy swords, the jeweled crowns, the wooden sailboats and rocking horse, the toy coaches...

The oldest explained, "It was s'posed to be the color of my Papa's and Ana's, but it wasn't, so we washed it."

Unfortunately, in their effort to eradicate their artwork, the eyes and mouth had faded along with the scrubbed head, but Merrick refrained from pointing out that fact.

The oldest daughter peered up at her father and, sensing his distress, sweetly offered him her free hand. Instinctively, she seemed to understand that he needed her tender touch. Rusty quietly accepted her loving offer, his eyes haunted in a way only a father's could be after losing a child.

Rusty robbed to feed his children—these children—and somehow that revelation muddied the line dividing right from wrong.

Staring down into the dirty, but lovely little faces of Rusty's three girls, Merrick was suddenly relieved he hadn't had Rusty arrested. It didn't make thievery right, but here and now, looking at his girls, it didn't seem entirely wrong, either.

Merrick was at a loss for words.

He wanted to know more about the daughter Rusty lost, but couldn't very well ask the man, not when he was certain he was already supposed to know.

Fidgeting, the middle child kicked her bare feet against the ground, turning Merrick's attention to the land Rusty seemed so grateful for, and Merrick examined the topsoil. It was thin and the ground was hard, nearly impossible to till. Poor Rusty must break his back only to coax a seedling from it.

Our sister Ana went to heaven, but we don't wanna go there yet...

Christ bedamned. His heart hurt over at the memory of those innocent words. Merrick wasn't sure how long he knelt there, examining the silt that sifted like sand through his fingers...contemplating his brother's involvement in these people's lives. It must have been only seconds, but it felt like hours.

His brother dirtied his hands for these people... in more ways than Merrick could imagine. This was his family's land; these people had likely relied upon his ancestors for support. These were not the sort of folk who traveled far from their homes. They were born and raised here, died here.

Ian must feel entirely responsible for them.

Merrick stood then, his view of the world somehow drastically skewed during those few seconds.

In Meridian, he sat within his nice, comfortable office, calculating investments and drinking port, completely oblivious to the fact that somewhere in the world, a child was dying of starvation, and there was something he could do about it.

Perhaps he couldn't save the world, but every life mattered.

"Katie, sweetling..." Rusty's voice broke. "Go now, take your sisters with ye. Let us talk."

"Yes, Papa," Katie said, seizing both younger siblings by the hands to lead them away. "Come on," she said sweetly, her childish voice curiously adult-like. She turned her big blue eyes toward Merrick and waved good-bye. The two younger sisters followed her lead. All three waved as they scurried away toward the house where their mother stood waiting upon the porch along with Chloe, watching from afar.

It occurred to Merrick as he watched the children go: this was a simple life, but Merrick could be happy if these were his own children and Chloe their mother. She stood there on the porch, completely oblivious to his scrutiny, hair blowing in the breeze, arms crossed and smiling fondly as she watched Rusty's children run giggling toward the house.

TANYA ANNE CROSBY

God's truth, if it would save their precious lives, he would steal for them, too.

He couldn't stand here and do nothing. He needed to contact Ryo and it occurred to him that there might be a way to kill more than one bird with a single stone.

A ring stone, to be precise.

If he could help it, Merrick intended to make certain they never had to steal again… except, perhaps, one last time. "I need you to do something for me," he told Rusty.

"Anything, Hawk," Rusty said without hesitation.

"Very good. This is what I need you to do…"

CHAPTER 9

"*A*n invitation?"

"Yes, Miss Chloe," said Aggie the following day. The staff was kept at a frugal minimum and each servant labored furiously to accomplish the long lists of tasks assigned to them. Aggie was one of the few who hadn't been dismissed.

"From who?"

"Lord Lindale!" Aggie exclaimed, giggling.

"You must be mistaken," Chloe said, confused.

The girl nodded enthusiastically, her youthful face aglow. "An invitation to dine!" She was no more than seventeen, Chloe surmised, and lovely with strawberry-gold curls and sun-kissed cheeks. She didn't mean to, but she gave the girl a frown for sounding so utterly delighted by the prospect.

Lindale had doubled her salary. Now he was wooing her. He must be after something, but what? What could he want from her? Chloe had nothing left of value to her name.

And why, pray tell, the sudden interest? He'd never spared her more than a few polite exchanges during the seven months she'd been in residence, and now, suddenly, he seemed to be pursuing her.

It didn't make sense.

Neither did the gooseflesh that erupted on her skin.

No, she couldn't possibly be flattered by the invitation. She refused to be bought. At any rate, even if he wanted nothing more than her company, she told herself, it didn't mean she could suddenly forget his previously sour attitude and general discourtesy.

"Thank you, Aggie," Chloe said, accepting the proffered envelope. It was sealed. Chloe furrowed her brow. "How did you know it was an invitation?"

Aggie gave an excited little nod. "Because 'e said so, Miss Chloe." She smiled winningly. "I really, really do think 'e likes you!"

Poppycock! Lindale only liked himself. Chloe's brow furrowed. He'd probably already used up every available woman in Glen Abbey, she thought to herself, and Chloe was to be his final conquest—or so he believed. Well, not if Chloe had any choice in the matter—and that was the one thing she did have. Choices. One always had choices, no matter the circumstances.

She tore open the invitation with a vengeance and sat upon the bed to read it. It read simply: "The Right Honorable the Earl of Lindale requests the pleasure of your company this evening for dinner. Please arrive in the foyer to be escorted at eight, prompt."

Chloe chewed her bottom lip. Damn and blast. She supposed it must seem a dream come true, a physician's daughter to be the invited guest of an earl. And Lindale was quite the handsome suitor, after all. He was absolutely adored by the ladies—all ladies—and his lineage was impeccable. He was, as some would say, a most eligible bachelor. But Chloe was not impressed. Indeed, he must have a motive, but what on earth could it be?

She couldn't very well refuse him.

Could she?

Should she?

A glance at Aggie found the girl awaiting her response with bated breath.

Chloe hated to disappoint.

If she embarrassed Lindale with a refusal, would he ask her to leave the manor? He was, after all, the true master of this house. It wasn't as though she wanted his affections; he couldn't hurt her any more than he already had. Besides, she was interminably curious.

"Very well. You may inform Lord Lindale it would be my pleasure." Though Chloe's tone was tinged with sarcasm, Aggie overlooked it and gave a little leap of joy.

She clapped her hands together. "What will you wear?"

Something like butterflies took flight in Chloe's belly. But it must be Aggie's enthusiasm that left her a wee bit giddy. As for a gown, she really hadn't much to choose from, but it didn't matter because this wasn't at all what it appeared. "I don't know," Chloe answered honestly, and laid the invitation down upon the bed, contemplating her choices.

Unbidden, the memory of his kiss assaulted her, and her heart flopped against her breast. Her face felt flushed and her palms slightly damp. She stood, fanning herself, trying to eradicate the taste of his mouth from her lips, the very memory of his embrace. "Perhaps I shouldn't go, after all," she said weakly. "I feel suddenly quite feverish."

Aggie giggled softly. "It's only nerves, Miss Chloe," she said, sounding suddenly far too mature. Another glance at the girl's face showed a very different Aggie. Something about the knowing look in her eyes made Chloe feel like the more naive of the two.

Chloe took in a breath and tried to clear her head.

There was so much to be done in so little time.

Zounds, but there must be something suitable she had to wear.

A sense of panic enveloped her, and she rushed to the wardrobe. Opening it revealed a meager assortment of garments that might have embarrassed her to wear in more finer households, but here, at Glen Abbey Manor, everything was old and overused. Even some of Lady Fiona's gowns were somewhat worse for the wear. Still, Aggie gasped with delight at the riches Chloe unveiled and Chloe felt an immediate twinge of guilt.

Chloe reached in, pulling out a very wrinkled dress of soft blue chiffon with ivory lace cuffing at the sleeve and hem. The neckline was fashionable but modest. She'd worn the gown to her cousin's wedding in Edinburgh two years past and there hadn't been an occasion to wear it since.

Aggie sighed wistfully. "Oh! It's beautiful, Miss Chloe! It's aboot time to stop wearing those mourning colors anyway." She held her hands out. "I will take it and press it at once."

Chloe wasn't accustomed to being waited upon. "Oh, no!" she said. "I don't mind doing it myself."

"But I insist!" Aggie said. "It'll be my pleasure, Miss Chloe. Anyway, you've your own duties to attend." She tried to take the dress from Chloe's hands and Chloe frowned.

"Well... thank you, I suppose," she said, reluctant to release the gown. It wasn't her place to utilize servants in such a fashion, and she was scarce more than a servant herself.

Aggie pulled the gown firmly from her grasp, smiling reassuringly. "It's a fine day, Miss Chloe, when one of *them* notices one of *us*. I desperately wish to do this, please."

Chloe sighed. "Very well," she relented, releasing the dress.

But, after all, she hated to disappoint Aggie; she was certain Lord Lindale hadn't romance on the mind, and she wanted to warn her not to get her hopes up.

Aggie didn't give her an instant to reconsider. The girl scurried out of the room with a flurry of blue chiffon trailing behind her, and the instant she was gone, Chloe wanted to race after her.

She simply couldn't do this.

She'd never dined with a man before—not alone. And come to think of it, never at all. Her father didn't count, and he'd never invited guests to their house. He'd worked hard and she had worked by his side, eagerly learning everything he would teach her. By the end of the day, it had been a blessing simply to enjoy a peaceful meal together.

It was Chloe's childhood dream to continue her father's practice, but it wouldn't be an easy goal to achieve because she wasn't a man and therefore could never formally study medicine. What she knew, she knew only because her father had respected her enough to teach her and because she'd pored over his medical journals. It was highly unlikely that she could take her skills to Edinburgh or to London. No one there would ever seek the care of a woman. Only in Glen Abbey was she free to pursue her dreams, but when she'd lost her house, she'd lost what little security a roof over her head had afforded.

Lindale, the cad, was a greedy penny-pinching thief who parted with his coin only to satisfy his own vices. That he'd agreed to double her salary was perfectly shocking, but Chloe would need to see it to believe it.

Hmm, she thought. Perhaps the fall knocked some decency into him. One could only hope. And yet, though Chloe couldn't put her finger on what it was about him that had changed, something irrefutably had.

Never in her life had anyone looked at her the way he had looked at her yesterday. He'd gazed at her with such—she couldn't describe it—unbridled hunger in his eyes that it made her shiver merely over the memory.

To her utter dismay, she couldn't stop thinking about it... the way he'd kissed her, the way he'd held her.

She wondered what he was doing... right now... and then wondered why she was wondering about what he was doing. The entire situation was unthinkable. What was the matter with her that she couldn't stop thinking about the man? Would she lose her head over any fool who dared steal a kiss from her? And yes, indeed, he had stolen from her yet again.

And yet, it must be true, because Lord Lindale was hardly the sort of man she admired or respected. He was nothing at all like Hawk. Hawk was everything she'd ever desired in a man and more—compassionate, kind, generous, courageous...

The heroic images she conjured in her head at the thought of the Highwayman made her shiver slightly.

They claimed he was tall, nearly six-foot-eight, and that he had once single-handedly offed six men. Chloe wondered if that were true. If it was, she was quite certain he'd had good cause, as he'd yet to harm a hair on the heads of his victims. The men he might leave rankled, but the women were left in a swoon of admiration. Yes, indeed, he was fodder for bed tales, and mothers recanted his stories to children as they closed their eyes each night. And sometimes, come morning, there would appear a brimming basket of goods on their doorstep... and lying beside the anonymous gift was the single, tiny white feather of a hawk. Children strung them and wore them as trophies about their necks.

No one knew precisely what he looked like because he wore that black hooded mask to hide his face. But a prostitute Chloe once treated, who worked at the Pale Ale, had encountered him more than once and she swore she'd spied him bareheaded. She'd said his smile was like a string of shimmering pearls and that his eyes were like gentle blue moons, bright and glowing with kindness.

Chloe sighed softly.

She'd come to fear there were no heroes left in the world. Only Lord Lindales. And she was a silly fool to hope for anything else.

He'd stood her up.

Bloody scoundrel!

What was worse, he'd sent his mother in his stead. Chloe fumed as she descended the stairs and saw Ian wasn't there. It was just like that cad to do something so vile. Was this how he intended to punish her for yesterday's insolence?

She took another step downward, trying to mask her flare of temper. As she made her way down, she straightened her shoulders and lifted her chin, denying herself even the smallest sliver of self-pity.

What had she expected?

She was heartily ashamed to admit she had actually been anticipating the evening. What a silly chit she'd been. She was acutely aware that Aggie had gathered all the servants; they were *all* peeking at her from behind their various hiding places. Even Edward, who was standing at the front door, was present to witness her dashed hopes.

"Before you go on cursing him," Lady Fiona said, smiling serenely. She put up a hand to silence Chloe when Chloe opened her mouth to deny it. "You must know Ian has quite a design for this evening."

He did?

Chloe's eyes must have revealed her doubt.

"It's true," Fiona insisted with a smile. "In fact, you should feel quite special, my dear. My son has gone through quite a lot of trouble to impress you."

Chloe didn't know how to respond. She couldn't imagine Lord Lindale worrying over impressing anyone. And she had been cursing him, for sure; she felt both duly chastised and a little disarmed by the revelation. She blinked. "Where is he?" Her voice sounded entirely too breathless even to her own ears.

"Never you mind," Lady Fiona said pleasantly. "You will need a pelisse," she added matter-of-factly. "I believe it's quite nippy outdoors."

Chloe's heart beat erratically as she continued to descend the staircase. She knew everyone was watching and dearly hoped she wouldn't trip over her one good dress.

"Come, my dear," Fiona commanded, wiggling a finger at her when Chloe hesitated.

Chloe's cheeks warmed under so much scrutiny. She felt a little as though she were on the fringes of a fairy tale as she completed her descent.

At last she stood before Lady Fiona, and with a critical eye, Lady Fiona assessed her gown. It was hardly anything worth fussing over, but Aggie had pressed it just so, and the airy fabric hung like whispers on her slim figure. Delicate ivory lace spilled from her cuffs and peeked out from beneath the airy hem. The blue of the gown was still as vivid today as it had been when new—but of course, it was. It had spent every moment inside a dark closet. Most certainly, it was the finest dress Chloe owned. It was the best she could do, but she had a sudden fear that Lady Fiona would find her lacking.

"Yes, I think this will do quite nicely," Lady Fiona approved, and she lifted her hand from her lap to reveal a glistening choker. She raised it for Chloe's inspection. Chloe gasped at the sight of it. It was a dazzling silver, with literally hundreds of tiny, winking diamonds and a few well-placed sapphires. She didn't know what to say. It was like nothing she had ever seen before—certainly unlike anything she'd ever worn. In fact, she didn't own a single piece of jewelry, save for the ring her mother gave her.

Lady Fiona held the choker out to her. "Oh!" Chloe said with an embarrassed gasp. "I mustn't—you shouldn't!" She shook her head.

"Rubbish!" Lady Fiona said firmly. "It was a gift to me from Ian's father and I would dearly love to share it with you, my dear. It will match quite nicely with your lovely blue dress."

Chloe's heart swelled with gratitude over Fiona's sweet compliment.

"This was a gift from Lord Lindale's father?" she asked with awe. How very generous of Lady Fiona to share it, but... good, lord! This was hardly anything she would have anticipated. Chloe hadn't the first clue what to say in response. Lady Fiona rarely spoke of her late husband. Now, she wanted to know more, though she daren't pry.

Lady Fiona's eyes betrayed a shimmer of moisture. "Yes, my dear. He gave it to me the night he asked my father for my hand in marriage."

Chloe furrowed her brows. She thought Ian's father was a merchant. How could such a man have possibly afforded such an extravagant gift? Nor had she understood that he'd asked for Lady Fiona's hand in marriage. Chloe could have sworn her father had said the two eloped.

"You cannot harm it. Go on, take it," Lady Fiona urged her.

Chloe reached to take it from Lady Fiona's hands and Aggie came scurrying out from the parlor at once. "I will help!" she said excitedly.

"Oh, thank you, dear," Fiona said to Aggie, smiling at the young woman. "I'm afraid I cannot manage from this infernal chair."

"It is… absolutely beautiful," Chloe said in disbelief, as Aggie lifted it before her, placing it about her throat, "Thank you so much!" She was enormously confused by the recent turn of events. In the space of a single day, nothing seemed at all the same. How could she suddenly feel so thrilled to dine with a man who only yesterday she'd claimed to despise?

What changed?

And when?

"You look radiant," Fiona said warmly when Aggie stepped away. She glanced at the timepiece that lay in her lap, and exclaimed, "Good grief! It's five after the hour! You must hie now."

Chloe blinked. *To where?*

"Go on now," Lady Fiona urged, waving a hand toward the door where Edward stood waiting. He turned to retrieve a snow-white pelisse from the coatrack and held it out for her. But the pelisse wasn't hers, and it was… entirely too… rich.

"Well, go on," Fiona commanded.

Chloe felt her feet move without direction.

Feeling suddenly surreal, as though everything were all happening in a dream, she allowed Edward to settle the pelisse over her shoulders. Without a word, he opened the front door and Chloe stepped outside to find a coach at the ready. Afraid to turn about for fear that everyone was still staring at her, she hurriedly climbed into the carriage, half expecting to find Ian waiting inside.

He wasn't there.

The carriage was entirely empty, save for a single red rose that lay upon the facing seat.

Chloe didn't touch it. She didn't dare. It didn't seem remotely possible it could be for her.

Nervously, her fingers sought the choker at her neck. It felt incredibly heavy and wickedly beautiful.

Sweet Lord, she felt beautiful simply wearing it— though merely one of its gems would feed a family for years.

Guilt pricked at her. It was more than she could bear. This was not her life, nor did she wish it to be. So why did it feel so... titillating?

If this was Lindale's idea of a joke, she would never forgive him. Only remembering the kiss, her hands unconsciously moved to her lips. God have mercy, the mere memory shouldn't make her belly flutter, but it did.

Would he kiss her again tonight?

No, certainly not. He wouldn't dare do it again— he'd promised—or had he? She had the sudden overwhelming desire to burst from the carriage and run.

Too late. The vehicle pitched into movement and lumbered down the long drive. For better or worse, Chloe was along for the ride.

CHAPTER 10

*H*oping for some insight into his brother's mind, Merrick listened quietly while the men bantered amidst themselves. There was an easy camaraderie between them and an optimism that didn't match their words. They spoke of death and hunger and yet ribbed each other with obvious good humor. One thing became clear: Poor as these men might be, they were contented. Merrick envied their easy attitudes and fellowship. All his life he'd enjoyed neither. He wondered how Ian became involved with them.

"Tell me again why we're robbin' your own bloody coach," one man asked.

"To divert suspicion, ye dolt," Rusty replied.

However, Merrick hadn't told Rusty the entire truth. He needed a way to introduce the ring to his mother without casting undue suspicion upon himself. He couldn't simply hand it to her. He hoped Fiona would feel alarmed by its presence—alarmed enough to reach out to his father. Merrick hoped she would call upon his father, though Ryo would intercept the message, he knew.

In fact, he was counting on it.

For his plan to work, Ryo had to be the one to receive the ring from his mother. As soon as Ryo realized he had the wrong brother, he would return for Merrick. It might be a long shot, but it was the only thing he knew to do without revealing himself.

He also intended to prove to Chloe that Ian's crusade was not entirely noble, nor was it the only option his brother had available to him.

Lastly, he'd told his mother about meeting Chloe for dinner and he knew she would adorn Chloe appropriately. Whatever booty he acquired tonight, he intended to give to these men and their families. Later, he would see that the value of the item was replaced. In the meantime, these men required food on their tables, and he didn't know any quicker way to achieve that goal. It was more than apparent he wouldn't get any funds from Edward—or from his mother, for that matter. Merrick's pockets were empty, and the clock was ticking. *Loudly.*

A vision of Rusty's three little daughters came to mind, dirty faces and shy smiles. What must it feel like to be part of a close family, to know your children intimately, to crawl into bed each night and hold your wife close?

He thought of Chloe and his loins tightened.

He couldn't imagine her retiring to her own chamber night after night... couldn't imagine her wishing to.

There had been no warmth between his parents. In fact, it seemed more oft than not that neither knew the other even existed. With a sudden sense of conviction, he decided he didn't want that for himself. He wanted to lay every night near his wife, holding her close, caressing her. And close on the heels of that thought came a stupefying revelation. Two days ago he hadn't even wanted a wife... now he wanted Chloe. He'd always gotten everything he'd ever desired, but for the first time in his life he didn't have the influence of his name and his money. So, if he wanted Chloe, he was going to have to win her. Whatever Ian had done previously clearly hadn't impressed Chloe. She was a strong woman who knew what she believed in and what she believed was that Ian was a cad and a rogue. Instead of swooning over him, she'd tossed down her gauntlet.

Merrick eagerly accepted the challenge.

"We aren't going to hurt 'er, are we, Hawk?"

They were talking about Chloe—again. Every man present objected when they'd discovered who was to be the occupant of the carriage.

"Of course not," he reassured them.

"Ye muckspout! That's why we've taken the bullets out of our pistols," Rusty reminded.

"And she won't know who we are?"

"Not unless you open your bloody mouth, Angus," answered Rusty.

Their concerns were beginning to chafe Merrick; it seemed to him that they were all a little too solicitous… almost as though they were all enamored of Chloe.

But he couldn't blame them.

He'd been enamored with Chloe from the instant he'd set eyes upon her.

"She's got a guid heart, that one," commented Angus.

"Aye," agreed another, "when my boy was six, she came tae stitch his head after 'e fell from the rooftop, and then she refused payment."

"Aye, well, she can tend me and mine any day," chimed Angus.

Christ on a pony, Merrick wouldn't mind hearing these tales—in fact, he wanted to hear them—but the tone of their voices as they discussed Chloe made him feel entirely too possessive. Not to mention that he felt acutely out of place among these men; his life was nothing like the ones they described. "What the devil was your six-year-old doing on the roof?" he asked the man.

"Fixing a leak," the man replied, then added matter-of-factly, "Mary, my wife, woulda helped, but she was already gone, bless her soul."

"And he'd hae done it himself," quipped Angus. "But, fat bastard that 'e is, he'd hae caved in his roof."

The men all laughed raucously, and Merrick felt instantly contrite for his snappish tone. It was obvious these people lived a difficult life.

In her own way, Chloe tried to help them. So did Ian, it seemed. But there must be another way.

As for the robbery, they'd chosen a spot on Glen Abbey Manor's parkland that was shielded by trees on every side. The road curved sharply through the grove. He hoped the carriage was traveling slowly, because he didn't want anyone to be hurt—most assuredly not Chloe.

Tonight there were five men aside from himself, not six. Donald Lowson remained with his wife whilst she gave birth to their firstborn child.

When he'd met these men, they'd all been nothing more than common, faceless thugs. Now they were men with lives and children and wives. It was obvious to Merrick that they held his brother in high esteem and would follow him blindly. Somehow, it didn't seem right that he knew they would die for him and he didn't even know their names.

Contemplating that fact, he watched the road for some sign of the approaching vehicle, uncertain how to proceed. It was, after all, his first robbery.

His heart flipped against his ribs once he spied the carriage coming around the bend. Nerves, he told himself. But he knew it was something more.

The thought of seeing her tonight, dressed only to

please him, made his blood burn like fire through his veins.

He alerted the men.

They gave him curious glances, but sat like warts on a frog, staring at him.

"Well, let's go get it," he said.

Still they sat, tilting their heads, regarding him with obvious confusion. He had the sense that they were waiting for him to do something, but for the life of Merrick, he didn't know what that could be.

The carriage was almost upon them.

Blast it all. If they didn't catch the vehicle in the grove, it would be much too risky to stop it out in the open field.

"Well?" prompted Rusty. "Aren't ye going to make the call?"

Merrick furrowed his brow. He hadn't a clue what the man was talking about. "Call?"

Rusty raised both brows. "The bird call—ye told us never to act unless ye gave it."

The memory came back to Merrick in a rush and another piece of the puzzle fell into place—the saker's call. Christ have mercy. He *had* heard it. It wasn't simply a figment of his imagination.

Ryo.

It must have been Ryo who'd introduced the saker to Ian. As his father's trusted servant, it made sense that Ryo would be a possible point of contact.

The men were still staring… waiting.

"Right," Merrick said, and then added, more to himself than to his men, "Never act without the bird call."

He put his hands together and attempted an imitation of the saker, and his men responded at once, flying toward the road to block the vehicle's path. They nearly trampled him in their haste. Stunned as he was, Merrick was the last to react.

. . .

CHLOE WAS SO deep in thought and so entranced by the rose left lying upon the seat that she didn't even realize they'd come to a halt until the door burst open.

She gave a startled little gasp at the sight of *him*.

It was Hawk!

For an instant she could only gape. So long she'd wanted to meet this man... and here he was, at last... flesh and blood... standing before her... robbing *her*.

The realization made her wince.

Her hand went to her throat, dreading what was to come. *Oh, no!* Lady Fiona had entrusted her with this precious necklace—Chloe shouldn't have accepted. Now what was she going to say when she faced Fiona?

Without a word Hawk offered her his hand, obviously intending for her to come out from the carriage, and realizing it was futile to resist, she gave him her hand and allowed him to assist her, all the while cursing herself for accepting the loan of Lady Fiona's jewels.

But as she alighted from the carriage, she felt a dizzying mixture of disappointment and excitement. This was, after all, the moment she'd been anticipating... to be able to tell Hawk in person how much she admired him, how great he was to take on this crusade in the name of the poor. In fact, if she could have, she would join his cause.

But Lady Fiona had become so dear to her heart. She didn't wish to disappoint her. She simply couldn't allow Hawk to take the necklace.

Dressed in black from head to his heels, his face concealed by a black hooded mask, he seemed to tower over her bigger than life. Behind the mask, only the curve of his lips and his eyes were visible, but it was enough to see that he was somehow pleased by the sight of her—or rather, by the sight of her necklace. His eyes glittered fiercely.

Chloe bemoaned her luck.

"Alas. These are treacherous times," he advised her very ominously when she stood before him. "It isn't wise for a beautiful young lady to travel alone at night."

Embarrassed by his veiled compliment, Chloe averted her gaze. Though she wasn't traveling precisely —she was still *on* the property. She wanted him to comprehend the risk he was taking by coming here tonight. Surely he must already realize. She gave him a meaningful look, brows arched and countered, "Neither is it wise to trespass on private property. These are Lord Lindale's parklands, sir."

"Am I trespassing?" He sounded completely unremorseful. He turned to his men. "Gentlemen, it seems we are trespassing."

The men all cackled at that, and Chloe felt her temper simmer beneath the surface.

"Yes," Chloe assured, trying to impress upon him the risk they were taking, "you are." If she didn't arrive soon, she was sorely afraid Lord Lindale would come searching for her and that would hardly be beneficial for anyone involved. "In fact, were I you," she advised, "I would leave before anyone discovers you are here."

"If you were me?" he said glibly, looking far too amused by Chloe's warning. "If she were me," he repeated to his men, as though they were not standing directly atop them. His lips curved a little arrogantly.

Chloe had to admit that it rankled a bit. She was, after all, only trying to save him from a round in gaol. She narrowed her gaze at him.

He said, and quite flippantly, "I suppose, then, if I must go, I shall have to take you with me."

Chloe's eyes went wide. "Surely you can't mean to ransom me!" He'd never done such a thing before.

He nodded. "If I must, then I must."

"That would gain you nothing!" Chloe assured. She shook her head adamantly. "I have no value! No one would pay for my return."

"What a pity," he told her and forced a sigh. "Then I will simply have to keep you."

"Sir!" she objected. "You cannot... *keep me*! I have duties and responsibilities!"

He sighed again, a long-suffering sigh. "Then I suppose I must make do with the lovely jewels adorning your beautiful throat. May I say they look ravishing tonight." But he wasn't looking at her jewels, she realized. He was looking straight into her eyes, and her heart skipped its normal beat.

Zounds! Was he flirting with her?

Well, of course he was flirting with her, she realized. He flirted with every woman he robbed—old and young, beautiful and hideous alike. That's why they all adored him. He was a gentleman thief!

At last, his eyes moved to her throat, or perhaps her bodice—Chloe wasn't certain. Her hand fluttered nervously to her throat and then fell to her breast, unsure what to conceal from his too forward gaze.

"Exquisite," he remarked, his voice low and raspy and Chloe was suddenly afraid to look at him. She averted her gaze, staring uncomfortably at his feet... very expensive boots...freshly polished. Evidently he kept some of the bounty for himself.

Annoyance flared once more.

She dared to peer up at him, wondering about the face behind that mask. His eyes had yet to leave her and it seemed to Chloe as though they undressed her, so intimate was his glance.

He bent closer and said, peering down at her bodice, "Do you, perchance... need assistance... removing them from your person?"

Her clothing? The question sent a quiver of alarm through her. "Assistance?"

"Do you need help," he snapped, "removing the deuced necklace?"

"Oh!" Chloe exclaimed, relief flowing through her. Her cheeks warmed with her chagrin. "No! You cannot have it, sir!" Her hand moved protectively to her throat, shielding the necklace from his greedy eyes. "I'm afraid it is not mine to give you! The necklace belongs to Lady Fiona, you see—a gift from her dear departed husband."

"Oh, really?" he said with a little more interest, and appeared somewhat moved by her plea. Perhaps she could persuade him to make an exception—just this once.

"Oh, yes! I would never forgive myself if I lost it. It's a rather precious necklace."

"Yes, I'm certain it is, but you haven't lost it. Rather, I plan to take it."

"You cannot have it." Chloe refused to remove her hand from her throat, unwilling to part with the jewels. It was a symbol of Lady Fiona's trust for her and she could simply not bear to disappoint her benefactor, nor could she allow this man to abscond with such a precious heirloom.

"Ah, but I'm not asking. "

A gun suddenly appeared between them and Chloe gulped at the sight of the barrel.

She peered up at the masked man who'd introduced it. He, too, had concealed his face, but his eyes clearly showed amusement at her expense.

Her temper fully ignited.

"You cannot have it!" she told him stubbornly, despite the gun in her face. Hawk had never once hurt anyone before; she didn't believe he would begin now, and she couldn't go back to Lady Fiona empty-handed. She started to remove her own ring from her finger.

"Here, you can have this instead. I'm afraid it's not gold or silver, but the stone must be worth something." She slid it off and offered it to Hawk.

He examined it in her hand without touching it, as though it were a distasteful bug. He arched a brow and asked rudely, "What the devil is that?"

Chloe straightened, wounded by his look. "It was my mother's. Please take it instead." It would ease her to know she had sacrificed the ring for a good cause.

He made no move to accept the gift, though she offered it willingly. "That, I'm afraid, is little more than a cheap bauble," he told her brutally.

It was not a cheap bauble!

His denigration chafed her. It was worth something —and to Chloe it meant a great deal more! "My mother gave that to me before she died," she informed him tautly, annoyed that he would discard her gift so readily. "What sort of crusader are you, anyway? Any gesture, great or small, should be duly appreciated," she lectured. Good night! He might be a savior to the townsfolk, but he was equally as rude as Lord Lindale!

She narrowed her eyes at him, studying him closer. In fact, he was about the same height as Lord Lindale. But it couldn't be.

She dismissed the possibility entirely. She simply couldn't imagine Lord Lindale resorting to something so low as to steal for money. He had money. Didn't he? He certainly seemed to spend enough of it on himself.

And besides, neither could she imagine him doing something so unselfish as to give it away to others.

"I'm afraid this wouldn't buy a mouse a scrap of cheese," he said, his tone amused at her expense, and entirely too familiar. "No thank you. The necklace, please…"

Chloe straightened to her full height, insulted by his outright refusal. She pushed the ring angrily back on her finger. "Well, I didn't say it was worth a king's ransom!"

She took a deep breath to compose herself. "I was simply trying to make up for the unfortunate fact that I cannot give you the bloody necklace. As I told you, it is not mine to give and I will not give it to you!" She stood her ground, glaring at the thief, her hand once again going protectively to her throat.

MERRICK WASN'T TRYING to insult her.

The look on her face as she'd offered the ring was so full of dismay over the possibility of losing it that he couldn't bring himself to accept it. But even if he had, he doubted any man present would allow him to do it. Standing before him now, her deep auburn hair shining under the moonlight, her cheeks a soft rose against her pale moonlit skin, she looked so adorably angry. He wondered what her hair would feel like gliding through his hands. He was sure it would be as soft as it looked… as must be her skin.

He knew those lips were sweet and he longed to kiss her.

And those velvety breasts… the rising curves beckoned to his mouth… and his hands. Good God, what must they feel like against his palm, the nipple pebbled against his flesh.

He wanted to bury his face in her sweet scent. *Roses.* He knew she would smell faintly of roses… like the one he'd left for her in the carriage.

Standing beneath the moonlight, her dress shimmering around her soft curves, the night fog swirling in delicate tendrils about her feet, she looked almost ethereal.

She was, indeed, an angel… as he'd believed at first glance.

A fiery angel.

His loins tightened, heat rushing through them.

Every encounter with her further enraptured him. She stood up to him in a way no woman—or man— ever dared. With the exception of Ryo. She offered him her own treasures, yet fought like a lioness to protect something that didn't even belong to her.

Damn, but she was beautiful tonight.

Too bad this had to be done; he needed that bloody necklace. He took the pistol from Rusty's hand and pointed it at her. "I'm afraid you have little choice in the matter, miss. Take the bloody necklace off, or I'll do it for you. And if I must do it, I cannot promise my hands will not wander."

She gasped aloud as the cold metal touched the bare flesh revealed by her décolletage. "How utterly rude!" she exclaimed, though her eyes showed a trace of fear.

He laughed softly, masking his regret. "Imagine that," he quipped to his men, "a rude thief."

PERHAPS THERE WERE ONLY A FEW, but it seemed a hundred, or more men, laughed at his jest.

Chloe bristled over his unremorseful tone. Tears pricked at her eyes. It did appear she didn't have a choice in the matter. The frigid barrel of his gun was a very rude reminder that this was entirely too real.

She realized only belatedly… half a dozen shadowy figures with gleaming silver in their hands surrounded her. They stood at a distance, their weapons glistening by the light of the moon. In her quarter, the coachman sat with the reins still in his hands, not daring even to look in their direction.

Och, but how could the evening have gone so wrong? Why, oh, why, had she agreed to this? What had she hoped to gain by accepting Lord Lindale's invitation? And where the devil was he?

Truly, even if she wanted Lindale—which she didn't —he was hardly the sort of man who would ever lower himself to wed a commoner. He would dally with them, certainly, but he had nothing to gain by wedding someone without money or title, and he wasn't the type to do anything lest it profit him.

Chloe had stupidly allowed herself to be carried away by the moment, by Aggie's enthusiasm, and her own vanity. At twenty-three, it had simply felt good to have a man notice her—even if it was Lord Lindale.

This town scarcely had a man remaining who was yet unattached. And even if there were some suitable bachelor, there were none who were suitable for her. She didn't wish to feel herself vain and trivial, because it wasn't so much that she felt herself too good to lower herself to being a farmer's wife, it was only that she couldn't quite relate to them. Thanks to her father, she aspired to more than simply shucking peas.

"The necklace," Hawk prompted, reminding her of the gun's presence with a cold kiss from its barrel against her cheek.

She peered up at Hawk, slow to respond despite the chill of metal against her flesh.

How had he known she would come this way? Somehow, he must have known. She cast the coachman a glance, studying his demeanor. He wouldn't even look at her.

Fear or guilt?

Hawk's gaze never left her as he waited for her to comply. Feeling utterly helpless, Chloe turned, giving him her back. "You'll have to take it from me," she told him, vowing not to aid him, though once she'd have leapt at the opportunity. "I won't simply give it to you!"

"Removing anything from your body would be my

utmost pleasure," he apprised her, handing his pistol to one of his men. Chloe swallowed as his hands worked to unclasp the necklace. Her heart beat a little faster as his warm fingers grazed her back. She swore she could feel the heat of his breath as he bent close to better see the clasp. And, once he removed the necklace from her neck, though she remained fully dressed, she felt completely vulnerable and exposed. With the weight of it relieved, she felt utterly stripped of her dignity and honor. Much to her dismay, she felt like weeping and she hadn't wept since her father died—and before that, when her mother passed away. As horribly as she'd felt when little Ana died, she hadn't even cried then.

It wasn't supposed to feel like this.

It wasn't supposed to make her feel as though she'd been violated. She knew what Hawk did with the money, knew it went for a good cause. And it certainly wasn't that she was so attached to that necklace that she couldn't appreciate the good it might bring to others, but she was, without a doubt, attached to her pride and honor, and somehow he'd reduced that to slivers. And she realized in that instant that if she could feel this way about something that wasn't even hers, how must others feel when he stripped them, unwillingly, of their personal possessions?

And yet, it could hardly be helped when there were far too many starving children in the world and too many oblivious people.

Could it?

Her heart felt too heavy to beat properly.

There must be some other way.

"Now... I have something for you," he revealed, and produced a crisp white kerchief.

Confused, Chloe stared at the offering, uncertain what he expected her to do with it. Dry her tears once he was gone? She glared at him, piqued by the insinuation that, like some schoolgirl, she would weep her eyes red once he left her. But though she might feel like it, she wasn't going to.

He held the kerchief out for her to take, opening his hand so she could better see it in his palm. It was then she realized that it was wrapped neatly about a small, rounded object.

Curious, she reached for it, but he snatched it away, "A little something for the lady of the house," he told her, "to make amends for the loss of her necklace. Tell her that it belonged to the occupant of the carriage I robbed some nights ago. He was rather insistent she receive it."

Chloe grit her teeth and turned her hand, waiting for him to hand her the kerchief. She wasn't going to allow him to tease her with it again. With narrowed eyes, she studied what she could of his face. His eyes were entirely too familiar to her...his mouth... that smirk...

He dropped the kerchief into her hand and her gaze fell to the tiny bundle. Whatever it was, it was small and heavy for its size—she tested its weight—like a ring, or a stone. It was probably only a rock—his idea of a joke.

She glowered at him.

"Now," he said, bowing gallantly, completely unaffected by her indignation. "I bid you good night, miss."

Before Chloe could anticipate his intent, he placed a gentle peck upon her lips. She shrieked furiously over the violation, but he didn't linger long enough to allow her to slap him for the shocking liberty. How dare he!

With a parting smirk, he gave a signal to his men to retreat. They were swift to obey. In less than an instant the night fog enveloped them all and she hadn't a clue in which direction they'd gone. They left her standing in the middle of the road with the white kerchief settled in her hand and the unmistakable taste of him upon her lips.

And suddenly, without a doubt, she knew the night had been carefully orchestrated. Lindale hadn't intended to woo her at all. No, he'd used her for some other design. Now, she fully intended to find out just what that was.

CHAPTER 11

*D*ismissing his men, Merrick hurried to the cottage before Chloe arrived. He'd purposely chosen her old cottage so he could surround her with familiar things. Now he hid the necklace in a vase, intending to dispose of it later. The mask he hid outside in the bushes. He'd gleaned enough information from Rusty to know that Ian had a jeweler in Edinburgh who bought stolen gems. It should be a simple enough task to find the man, though he felt a pang of guilt after what Chloe had revealed to him.

Curious about the necklace, he retrieved the vase from the mantel upon which he'd placed it, and lifted the necklace from within, inspecting it.

Had his father truly given the necklace to his mother? Had she kept it all this time? If she loathed him so much, wouldn't she have rid herself of the memory entirely—sold it for whatever money she could get from it, particularly considering the condition of the manor? It was in deplorable condition.

Evidently, the necklace meant something to Fiona, or she wouldn't have presented it to Chloe to wear tonight. Her affection for Chloe was more than apparent.

Did his mother love his father still?

Merrick studied the necklace critically. It seemed familiar to him somehow. Distinct as it was, there could not be another like it, he was certain. And then it occurred to him where he'd seen it and the significance of its presence here was unmistakable. There was only one woman Merrick had ever seen his father publicly acknowledge his affection for—his own mother. In one of the paintings that graced the portrait gallery in Meridian, this necklace adorned his grandmother's neck. God's bones! His father had truly loved Fiona. If the sheer number of his letters wasn't proof enough, this necklace surely was.

Could the two love each other still?

After all these years?

If so, how could his father have abandoned them?

Unless he hadn't the first clue what their circumstances were. His father's pride was such that if he felt they were well taken care of he wouldn't extend himself. Which led Merrick to believe that whomever handled the books for Glen Abbey was someone his father trusted... completely.

Edward.

However, if that were the case, he couldn't comprehend why Glen Abbey Manor would have no funds available.

Even if their rents and investments were scarce, his father was not a cruel man. Whether he loved Fiona or not, he would have taken responsibility for his child. But it was clear to Merrick that his father loved her desperately still. Had he strangled Glen Abbey's finances to force her to come crawling back to him? It was not his father's style, but it was certainly a possibility. Men—and women—did strange things in the name of love. And it had become rather obvious that there was much he didn't know about his father.

At the moment he scarce knew himself, if the truth be known. But he wondered, instead of simply giving Fiona the letter he'd stolen from his father, what if he could bring the two of them face-to-face?

One thing was certain, Merrick wasn't his father. He knew what he wanted, and he intended to go after it. He didn't intend to sit by and bemoan his loss for the rest of his days.

He started to replace the necklace within the vase and then decided that wasn't the best place to hide the jewels. In fact, it was the most obvious place someone might look. He took the necklace into the bedroom, where he doubted Chloe would step a foot, and found a suitable spot beneath the mattress. He tucked the covers back into place—just in time, as he heard the carriage wheel into the drive.

He scarcely had time to meet her at the door.

The very instant the carriage came to a halt, Chloe burst from it like a raging blue flame, her blue-chiffon dress flowing about her as she marched toward him. Her cheeks were a deep, angry rose and her delicate throat was unadorned, but for the flush that deepened her lovely skin.

She showed him the kerchief in her hand. It remained neatly bound. Obviously she hadn't bothered opening it. "You'll not believe what I have been through," she exclaimed, and suddenly, surprisingly, burst into tears.

Merrick didn't know what to do. He hadn't had much experience with weeping women. Patting her gently on the shoulder, he led her into the cottage.

It was all Chloe could do not to rage at him for his deception. And he'd brought her to her own cottage— the one he'd stolen from her—what a horrid slap in the face! But she realized she must keep her head to expose him.

The cottage was extraordinarily small compared to the manor. Since the repossession, it was rumored that Lord Lindale sometimes used it for his dalliances—a matter that somewhat disgusted her.

So he meant to seduce her, did he?

That fact made her all the more furious and she cast him a narrow-eyed glance.

The cottage was simple but quaint. Inside, it was elegantly decorated and well-kept, though it remained largely unoccupied. Nothing remained of her old life here. The interior had been gutted and remodeled to suit Lord Lindale's taste. Once a week, servants came to thoroughly scrub it and place fresh flowers in the vases —just in case guests were to be entertained.

Tonight, dozens of candles were lit about the main room—an extravagance in itself, for it was obvious by the sweet scent that they were made of beeswax. The manor used tallow, which left a thin layer of soot on everything. The servants dusted furiously to keep the furnishings free of it. Unlike the manor, the draperies here were new and bright, and the furnishings fashionable. Seeing the disparities only validated what she'd always believed about Lord Lindale—that he was a wastrel and a rogue.

And yet, how could that be entirely true if, in fact, he was Hawk?

Chloe looked about, chafing at the answer. Because he spent the money, not on the poor, but on himself. That much was apparent. So he gave a token bag of coins occasionally—that certainly didn't qualify him for sainthood.

Rotten scoundrel.

The hearth was ablaze, bathing the room in warm, flickering light. Together with the candles, it made a stunning effect. A small table in one corner sat elegantly adorned with crystal and porcelain. Lilies of various colors filled the vases surrounding it.

If Chloe didn't know better, she might have thought he'd meant to impress her. But he was only using her. She knew that as well as she knew the taste of his mouth—that thought made her face burn. She shouldn't know it at all.

He led her into the living area, toward the hearth.

What if she were wrong? What if he wasn't Hawk?

Chloe chewed her lower lip. If she was, indeed, correct, then the jewels should be hidden somewhere in this cottage. It was her task to find them.

Acutely aware of his hand on her arm, she cast him a surreptitious glance, noting the concern in his face, and quickly averted her gaze lest he see her thoughts. She sat upon the chair nearest the hearth and then set the kerchief in her lap.

"Tell me what happened," he demanded.

Chloe wiped the last traces of tears from her eyes. "I believe you know, my lord."

He knelt before her, his hand gripping the arm of her chair as he peered into her face. Chloe stared at his strong, lean hand, unable to look into his eyes, trying to determine if it was the same hand that had only a short time ago held a pistol to her cheek. "Tell me what happened, Chloe," he demanded once more.

Hearing her name spoken so intimately took her momentarily aback. "I—I was robbed," she said, peering up at Lindale, her heart beating a little faster.

"Hawk?"

Chloe nodded, watching his face for some expression that would betray him. She started to weep again in earnest. Was she so desperate for someone in her life, so lonely, that she would leap at any attention cast her way? And if she was wrong about Lindale, then she had, indeed, lost Lady Fiona's jewels and she would never, ever forgive herself. She should have leapt upon that man's ankles and refused to let him go.

Good night, but he was particularly dashing this evening, dressed in a black coat and trousers. His high cheekbones and chiseled face were striking by the light of the fire. And his lips... the very sight of them made her heart race a little faster. Ignoring the sound of her heart beating in her ears, Chloe glanced down at his boots.

They were the same sort of boots Hawk wore.

"I'm afraid you were right," she relented, narrowing her gaze at him. "Hawk is not a very nice man."

He arched a brow at her. "I tried to tell you so, Chloe. Thievery is not a noble pursuit." He placed his hand over hers, patting it gently. "I am sorry I wasn't there to protect you," he apologized, sounding entirely too sincere. "We should have ridden together, but I wanted you to feel like a princess tonight."

Chloe furrowed her brows. "I shouldn't have come at all. I don't belong here."

He said nothing for a moment, and then, "But I am pleased that you did." And he gently squeezed her hand.

Chloe narrowed her gaze at him. "If you mean to try to seduce me, it won't work." But she wasn't certain it was the truth, because he was seducing her already with only his look and sweet words.

She shivered as she stared into his eyes... they were so blue...like big blue moons.

His tone was soft when he spoke again. "I asked you here, Chloe... because I've wanted you from the moment I met you."

What? He'd barely acknowledged her when she'd come to live at Glen Abbey Manor. How could she believe anything he said now? Everything she knew about him seemed to be a lie.

"I don't believe you," Chloe said, shaking her head. "You were scarcely cordial when I arrived."

He lifted her hand up, kissing it gallantly, and said, "Will you believe me when I tell you I am not the same man you knew then?"

Chloe arched a brow at him. That was an understatement. She could well believe he wasn't the same man anyone knew.

They exchanged a long glance and then he released her hand and gestured to the bundle in her lap. "What is that?" he asked, then teased her with a wink. "Did you bring me a gift?"

"I don't know what it is," Chloe lied. "I haven't opened it yet. Hawk gave it to me to give to your mother. He said it belonged to the occupant of the carriage he robbed a few nights ago and that Fiona was to have it."

"Really?" His attention was obviously piqued. His brows lifted and he eyed the bundle with renewed interest. "It seems as though Hawk has been quite the busy thief of late."

"Indeed," Chloe agreed.

"I wonder what it is."

"Shall we open it?"

"Yes, of course. I would not blindly hand a gift from a thief to my mother."

Chloe nodded in agreement. She braced herself for his reaction. And without further ado, she picked up the bundle and handed it to Lord Lindale. "Then I shall allow you the honor, my lord."

He smiled slightly as he took the kerchief from her. Struggling with the knot, he wove it loose at last. When it lay open before them, he cast her a stupefied glance.

"I-It's a ring," he said, stumbling over his words.

Chloe understood why.

It wasn't the same ring originally placed within the

kerchief. This one was hers and the ruby with the strange crest was tucked safely where he would never venture... between her breasts. A sense of satisfaction came over her as he stared at the ring lying upon the kerchief. His jaw dropped only slightly. He seemed to wish to say something and then closed his mouth again, having said nothing at all. He touched his brow, pausing perhaps to think, and then looked at her with narrowed eyes.

MERRICK PURSED his lips as he studied her.

She knew.

The little shrew knew who he was.

Or... though it didn't seem her style, perhaps greed had gotten the better of her. In itself, the ruby with the Welbourne family crest engraved on its belly was worth an ungodly fortune—never mind the gold karats that encased it.

He felt her gaze narrow upon him and wondered what to say. There didn't seem much he could say without revealing himself. He scratched his head and then raked his fingers over his jaw as he stood.

He must search the carriage. She would have left the ring in the carriage, he was certain.

But perhaps this was, somehow, a test?

He lifted the ring from her lap and examined it. He asked as casually as he was able, "You say Hawk said it belonged to the occupant of the carriage?" It had been dark outside, but he was certain this ring was hers... the very one she'd tried to give him instead of his mother's necklace. A quick glance at her finger revealed her own ring was gone. "I must wonder...why should this particular ring concern my mother?" he contemplated aloud.

Chloe peered up at him, looking entirely too innocent for his liking. The tone of her voice was far too sweet. "I couldn't say, my lord." She shrugged. "It seems an ordinary ring."

Merrick pocketed the ring. "I suppose we shall find out soon enough. Shall we go now?"

Her expression turned instantly to one of alarm. "Go where, my lord?"

"Back to the manor," he suggested. "To give the ring to my mother."

"Oh, but no!" she exclaimed, bolting to her feet. "We can't go yet!"

"Why not? It's obvious that Hawk has ruined the evening for us already."

"Oh, but it's not ruined!"

Merrick arched a brow, challenging her. "Is it not?"

She sat back down and said in a small voice, scrunching her brow, "Not entirely." She tilted her lovely face at him and said in a rush, "My lord, I simply can't face her yet—not without the necklace. It was your father's gift to her."

Merrick frowned. He hoped she was squirming in that chair by the fire, because she would surely burn in hell for her lies.

"Very well. But I should, at least, send a message with the coachman." He told her firmly, "Stay here. I shall return in a thrice."

Rotten little liar.

Merrick spun on his heels and left her to wonder about his intentions, fully intending to search the coach, top to bottom.

If she had that ring, he intended to find it.

THE VERY INSTANT Chloe was alone, she leaped up from the chair, knowing full well she had precious little time to search the cottage before he returned. There was no time to waste. The vase was the first place she looked. Next, she checked the desk. Nothing. Her heart tripping painfully, she stood in the middle of the living area and asked herself... if she were a thief, where would she hide a precious necklace?

She doubted he would hide it in the kitchen—that was alien territory for a man. Her best bet, she feared, was the bedroom, though she dreaded walking into it. Like a spider's web, the very thought of entering there made her tremble slightly. But she was desperate to find the necklace.

Off to the bedroom, she went.

The master's room was impeccably neat, with nary a hair on a brush left to catch the eye. Chloe knew she would need to search thoroughly but quickly, lest he catch her. She set to work, looking high and low.

CHAPTER 12

The bloody ring was nowhere to be found.

Merrick checked even the closed bud of the rose he'd given her, thinking she might have slipped the ruby within. It wasn't there; it wasn't anywhere. *Hell and damnation!* Either she tossed the bugger out the carriage window or it remained on her person. But though he'd seen glimpses of her fiery temper, he knew she wouldn't have cast so valuable a piece, so that left one place to search…

He raked a hand over his face.

Christ almighty, this wasn't just any ring. Passed down from father to son for over three hundred years, it bore the Welbourne family crest. Merrick would be giving it to his own son someday. Ryo would have known instinctively that Merrick would never part with it—not at any cost—and he would have taken its delivery as a call for help. If Fiona knew anything of its value—and he was certain she did—she would have known not to part with it until Ryo arrived to claim it.

What did little Miss Chloe intend to do with that ring? What did she know?

The little vixen.

Cursing, he left off searching the deuced carriage. A

third perusal would be a wasted effort. She was probably already concealing the ring somewhere within the cottage... so she could return for it later. *Damn.* This evening wasn't going at all as he'd planned.

She wasn't in the living area when he returned. He checked the kitchen; it was empty, as well. Which left only two possibilities. It was a small cottage. Either she'd managed to slip out while he'd been searching the carriage and was halfway to Edinburgh by now—he knew she no longer had familial ties in Glen Abbey—or she was in one of the two bedrooms.

He made directly for the master's bedroom.

He found her there, standing before the oval mirror, casually brushing her hair.

The vision was such an intimate one that it took him momentarily aback. For a befuddled instant he couldn't even remember why he'd been searching for her to begin with, so entranced was he by the sight of her.

Her dark auburn hair was swept down, framing her lovely face. The ends of her long, silky hair curled gently... like a lover's finger atop her breasts. Her skin was flushed from the curve of her breasts to her beautiful cheeks. He swallowed. Hard. And he had to remind himself to breathe.

"Oh!" she exclaimed, catching sight of him in the mirror. "My lord!" She spun to face him when he entered, pretending to be startled by his sudden appearance. "I—I hope you don't mind terribly," she said, her voice betraying a slight quiver. "My pins were giving me a dreadful megrim."

Merrick still couldn't find his voice to speak.

"I'm sorry," she said, looking coy. "I shouldn't have... it's only that... I know I looked horrid with my hair a mess and tear stains on my face."

She looked anything but. She was ravishing.

Merrick's mouth felt suddenly parched; he licked lips gone dry. His loins tightened to the point that he hoped she wouldn't lower her gaze. No trousers could confine the greedy beast stirring there.

He cleared his throat. "Not at all," he managed to say. He forced himself to remain at the door, lest he go to her, lift her up, throw her down on the bed and take her like some crude barbarian. He was that bloody aroused.

She wasn't like the ladies of the *ton*, who gasped by day at the very thought of entering a man's boudoir, but secretly slipped between his sheets by night.

Nor, evidently, was she some shy miss.

He remembered the way she'd peeked beneath his coverlet when she'd thought him asleep and experienced a sudden violent wrenching of his gut at the thought of her lying with some other man.

He had to know—as badly as he needed to find that ring—if she was still a virgin.

She shouldn't have ventured into his bedroom, he thought darkly. Merrick considered himself a gentleman, but he was no saint and she'd changed the rules of the game when she'd entered his lair. Still, he daren't move too quickly. Like a tiger in a crouch, he waited for the right moment to pounce.

"You look radiant," he said, and meant it, his voice sounding thick even to his own ears.

CHLOE'S HEART began to thump wildly.

She hadn't found the necklace, of course, but she knew it must be here somewhere. Looking into his stormy eyes, she realized her foolishness. She heard the clip clop of her carriage fading away and realized he'd sent the carriage off; she was alone with him now.

The hungry intensity in his eyes was the same as it

was the morning he'd kissed her. His eyes were like blue flickering flames and his gaze, where it touched her, lit her body slowly afire. Her skin prickled with something like fear as he took a step nearer, but it wasn't precisely fear, she acknowledged. She swallowed the knot that arose in her throat and with a mind for self-preservation, took a step backward.

"Tell me... what are you really doing here, Chloe?"

She gulped deeply at the sensual sound of his voice, low and throaty. Her breathing grew heavy and her body convulsed in secret places. "M-my lord?" she said, feeling as though she would swoon under his scrutiny. His presence filled the entire room. "You invited me... remember?"

"To dine, yes, I know," he finished for her. "I meant... what are you doing in my bedroom?" He took her ring out of his pocket, made a point to look it over, then walked past her to the night table, eyeing her as he set the impostor ring down on the table.

Chloe watched him with a growing sense of alarm.

Why didn't he ask about the real ring?

If he did, she would return it straightaway. She'd only wished to know the truth.

He was closer now and she had the impression that it was by careful design. He watched her closely as he said, "I sent a message to the house that you've been robbed. The constable should be alerted at once."

Chloe's eyes went wide. She hadn't even thought about the constable. She knew the man would leap at the opportunity to interrogate her. It seemed to Chloe that he wished to catch Hawk more than he wished to breathe. What should she tell him? What if she were wrong about Lord Lindale? What if he was not Hawk, after all?

He must be bluffing, she decided, and straightened

under his regard. She refused to be cowed. If he was playing games, she could do the same.

"Good," she said, nodding, but her tone wasn't entirely convincing even to her own ears. She was a horrid liar. Even now, the cold metal ring stung the flesh between her breasts, and she longed to pluck it out and cast it at him accusingly. Heaven help her, she should never have come here to begin with. She should have gone back to the manor.

But... she couldn't stop staring at him, despite knowing it was a dangerous game she played. His gaze locked upon her face, his eyes entrapping her, and for the longest moment of Chloe's life, they stood staring at one another.

And she knew...

He knew.

Her heart beat like thunder against her breast. Her hand dropped helplessly at her side, the brush slipping to her fingertips. He closed the distance in the blink of an eye and came and took it from her, tossing it on the bed.

Chloe suddenly couldn't breathe.

"My God," he whispered. "You are so lovely." His fingers slid through her hair, pausing at her cheek.

Chloe's head fell backward at the shocking intimacy. She found it impossible to swallow, though she tried. As his hand cupped her face, she sucked in a breath. Why was she responding so wantonly? Why was her body behaving so traitorously? She was already seduced, she feared, and he had barely touched her.

No man had ever affected her so strangely.

Was she so hungry for the touch of another human being that she would lower herself to such behavior?

She lapped at her lips. "My lord," she protested, but it sounded more like a sigh when it passed through her lips.

"Chloe," he said, and it sounded like a plea. "I realize I promised I wouldn't, but I long to kiss you," he said, his tone sounding tortured. His arm went about her waist, drawing her fully against him. "Tell me you want me to."

Chloe's lips parted, but no words came. Her heart pounded so fiercely she knew he must hear it, as well. She melted against his embrace, closing her eyes, trying to summon the will to resist.

"I need to kiss you," he whispered hoarsely.

But kissing him would gain her nothing, Chloe reminded herself.

Loving him could lose her everything.

"If you tell me you don't want me to, I won't." His face touched her cheek, his lips lightly brushing her skin.

Chloe clung to him, her fingers clutching desperately at the sleeves of his shirt.

"But dear God help me, I've wanted you from the instant I saw you," he whispered. His arms locked about her waist, the hunger apparent in his embrace.

Chloe wasn't a child. Her father never treated her as most fathers treated their daughters. He'd never sheltered her from truth. She knew what kisses led to. But Heaven forgive her for being so wanton, she needed him to kiss her, too. She nodded almost imperceptibly, but he must have felt her because his lips closed over hers in that instant. He pressed his mouth against hers so tenderly, so delicately, that Chloe could only moan in response.

He was an earl, she told herself desperately. This was foolish... she *must* stop... but her lips would not obey.

"So sweet," he whispered against her mouth, and Chloe felt his words throughout her body; the blood warmed through her veins and her breasts tautened until they ached. She gasped softly for breath as his tongue swept over her lower lip. She was drowning in desire… felt with parts of her body she didn't know could feel.

MERRICK'S BODY responded with an explosion of desire.

It had been so long since he'd lain with a woman—so long since he'd wanted to. But she wasn't merely some woman… she was a rare flower and he never wanted her to wilt—never wanted to be the cause of it. By her response to his kiss, timid, but eager, he knew it would be so easy to lay her down… right here upon the bed and take her… but he couldn't… not yet.

He wanted her not merely willing, but forever.

If he violated her now, she would regret the hastiness of their loving. And yet… if he walked away now, it also meant he couldn't search her for the ring.

It was a matter of priority. The ring or Chloe?

Instead of taking it, he would have to coerce it from her…make her want to give it to him. For that, he needed her trust.

Knowing he would pull away after one last taste of her, he drank deeply of her mouth, feeding from the sweet nectar, and then, reluctantly, tore himself away, thoroughly ignoring the throbbing of his loins.

He couldn't be alone with her tonight.

He couldn't be trusted, he realized.

Aside from that, he couldn't trust her to remain in the vicinity of the necklace.

HIS WITHDRAWAL LEFT Chloe feeling both relieved and dashed.

If he hadn't been holding her so tightly, she might

have crumpled at his feet, so dazed was she by his passionate kiss.

"I'm certain you're not in the mood for an elaborate dinner after the ordeal you've been through," he suggested, sounding suddenly curt. "The carriage will return soon." He turned her to the bedroom door and gave her a gentle shove toward it.

Stunned by his sudden, obvious dismissal, Chloe allowed him to lead her out of the room.

Panic filled her.

No! She couldn't leave yet!

She certainly couldn't leave the cottage without finding that necklace! "But I'm ravenous!" she lied.

"Not to worry," he countered. "I'll see you safely home and then have a meal sent to your room."

There was nothing Chloe could say to that. His tone brooked no argument. She hadn't the first notion what she'd done, but it was evident by his demeanor that he no longer wished Chloe to remain in his presence.

True to his word, it wasn't long before the carriage returned—or perhaps it had never left. Chloe was too confused to know. Lord Lindale saw her aboard, then returned briefly to the cottage. Chloe suspected she knew why, but said nothing as he boarded the carriage and sat in the facing seat.

He lifted up the rose before settling himself and handed it to her with a slight smile. "This, my love, belongs to you."

But his look did not match his sweet words.

He'd called her my love.

Could it be that he used sweet words for every woman he knew? At least for those from whom he wanted something?

Or had he meant it?

CHAPTER 13

*T*hat night, Chloe lay in bed twirling the rose in one hand, the ring in the other.

The evening had managed to thoroughly confuse her.

It seemed to her that Ian MacEwen—Lord Lindale —was not at all the man she'd supposed he was. She'd discovered more about him during the past week than she had in all the months she'd been in residence. And what she discovered was that he was full of secrets.

Had his wastrel attitude been entirely an act from the first day she'd met him?

Since his youth, Lindale was said to have had a greater taste for women than he did for his whiskey. Her belly turned at the thought of him wooing other women. It gave her a twinge of some emotion she daren't confess to—jealousy?

Surely not.

Gossip would have it that he frequented every unseemly pub in the Glen Abbey vicinity, flouting in the face of propriety. Chloe had to wonder now if that had merely been a cover for... other activities.

Could it be that he hadn't wanted her presence at

Glen Abbey only because he hadn't wanted her to un-mask him?

Still, something about the situation did not add up.

I've wanted you from the instant I saw you...

Could it be true?

His words clung to her brain like the taste of him upon her lips.

At first Chloe had been invited to take her meals in the dining hall, along with Lord Lindale and his mother. Lord Lindale had repeatedly declined to join them, and then, the one-time Chloe did not join them, he'd returned to the table. It sent a clear message to her that she wasn't wel-come, and from then on she'd declined to join them ever.

Aside from that, however, he'd never actually mis-treated her. In fact, he'd scarcely even talked to her. Like Edward, he'd barely acknowledged her presence.

But now he claimed he'd wanted her from the in-stant he'd spied her. It simply didn't ring true. The fall from his horse had obviously, in truth, rattled his lying brain, so that he no longer knew what was true and what was not.

She inhaled the sweet scent of the rose he'd given her and then set it upon the night table, turning her at-tention to the ring in her hand.

By the moonlight she studied its design. The stone was a richly colored ruby that bore the etchings of a family crest on its belly. She couldn't see it now in the dim light, but she knew it was there. The ring itself was gold and it, too, bore intricate carvings that were unfa-miliar to her.

Why had he given her this ring to give to Lady Fiona? Would Lady Fiona recognize the jewel? And why hadn't he simply handed the ring to his mother instead?

Chloe considered her best course of action. Should

she give the ring to Lady Fiona? Or should she use it to draw out Hawk? She fell asleep devising a plan.

LADY FIONA TOOK the news well.

She assured Chloe that the loss of the necklace wasn't her fault, but Chloe felt entirely responsible. She fully intended to see to its return, no matter the cost. She didn't dare bring up the ring, but Lord Lindale did, indeed, give his mother Chloe's ring—which only made Chloe wonder if she weren't mistaken. Perhaps he wasn't Hawk. The entire situation was simply confusing.

But, as they sat in the drawing room examining the strange gift, Lindale seemed properly perplexed by the ring's significance. He scarcely looked at Chloe. His mother wasn't able to shed any light upon it, either, but Lady Fiona cast Chloe a questioning glance.

Chloe's face burned hot under Lady Fiona's quick scrutiny. Judging by her expression, Fiona must realize the ring belonged to her. But she never revealed as much to Lord Lindale, and Chloe was beginning to feel Glen Abbey Manor was a house full of impossible secrets.

Later, after Fiona was settled in the garden, Chloe slipped out of the manor and ventured into town.

The one person she knew who'd connected with Hawk was Emily. Chloe sought her out, discreetly sending a young lad into the Pale Ale to ask Emily to meet her in the alley.

Emily emerged from the inn almost at once, her slim hips swaying beneath a faded blue dress. Her dark hair was pinned atop her head in a haphazard fashion. She was a lovely girl, not more than seventeen, but she looked and behaved older than her years. Life had dealt her a brutal hand; the lass had been on the streets since the tender age of twelve. But Emily was obviously quite pleased to see her; she gave Chloe an eager embrace, then stepped back to examine Chloe. She said, without a trace of envy in her voice, "You always look so nice, Miss Chloe."

Chloe thanked her, but she was anxious to enlist her aid and came directly to the point. "Remember how you told me you'd met Hawk?"

"Aye," Emily replied with a wink and a grin, eager for the opportunity to tell her romantic tales of the highwayman.

"I need you to get a message to him for me. It's urgent. Do you think you could do that?"

Emily's smile faded. She shrugged noncommittally, her expression suddenly uncertain. "Miss Chloe... I don't know... you know I'm always grateful for your help, but I really don't know if I should."

"Oh, please! You must!" Chloe urged. If she must call in every favor in her effort to find Hawk, she would.

"He's like the wind," the girl said dramatically, waving her hand in a breezy fashion. "No one can find him, he must find you," she explained.

Chloe leaned close to whisper to the girl. "Emily, please, you must help me. You're my only hope."

Emily gave her a troubled look.

Chloe sensed the girl wished to help, but her loyalties obviously belonged elsewhere.

"I'm hoping that... with all your..." she searched for a kinder word "...affiliations, you must know someone who knows how to reach him," she reasoned.

Emily twisted her lips. "I don't know," she said again, but Chloe suspected she knew much more than she was admitting. "But for you, Miss Chloe... I will try."

"That's all I ask," Chloe said, relenting. "Please,

please tell him I have something he lost, and I wish to return it."

Emily's eyes lit up. "I see, so you wish to help him?"

Chloe nodded and withdrew a coin from her reticule as a gesture of thanks. She handed it to the girl. "If you only try to get that message to him, that is truly all I ask." Then, to ease the girl's conscience, she added, "If you cannot, I will not be upset." But she knew, somehow, by the look in Emily's eyes, that Hawk would, indeed, get her message.

THE CARRIAGE WHEELED its way through nearly empty streets.

Merrick hadn't the first notion where he was going, only that he needed to be away from the manor to think. This town was hardly thriving, he realized. Nary a soul was anywhere to be found. For that matter, he hadn't seen Chloe since they'd presented Hawk's gift to Fiona.

Of course, his mother hadn't had the first inkling what to make of Chloe's ring, but something in her expression had given Merrick the impression that she knew far more than she'd let on about Ian's endeavors. She'd given Merrick a questioning glance, as though she'd expected him to supply the answer to the ring's meaning. But Merrick had only given Fiona Chloe's ring to divert Chloe's suspicions. Now, he was almost glad that Chloe stole the real ring, because he may have just given away the goose if, indeed, his mother knew about Ian's misadventures.

Oh, what a tale we weave...

Chloe, for her part, had been guiltily silent, unable to look at either his mother or at Merrick. She'd fled their presence the instant she was able.

Last night had been the most difficult thing he'd ever had to do… walk away when he'd wanted nothing more than to make Chloe his own.

She was beginning to occupy his every waking thought. He couldn't think straight anymore. Even his purpose at Glen Abbey had somehow become skewed.

As he passed the inn, a skinny young girl with ratty hair beckoned to him. The look on her face had been almost desperate, though she was as discreet as possible in her summons. She disappeared into the tavern.

Curious, Merrick rapped upon the carriage roof and bade the driver pull over.

One glance into the smoky bar gave him the impression that every male in town was here with his whiskey and a smoke. He took a seat at a table and the ratty-haired girl came quickly to serve him. "The usual, my lord?" she asked coyly.

Merrick raised his brows.

Damnation, there mustn't be much to choose from in this terminally ill town. That, or, Ian wasn't too picky about the company he'd kept. He nodded at the girl and prayed she was speaking of serving something other than herself.

She left him at once, returning momentarily with a stout glass of whiskey. The stinging scent of it cleared his nostrils even from where it sat upon the table. Bloody hell, his brother must have a stomach made of steel. He withdrew payment for the girl, and she smiled as she bent to quickly whisper something into his ear.

Merrick arched a brow when she was through speaking. "Really?" he asked, surprised.

The girl nodded.

He grinned and crooked a finger at her, luring her closer. "Tell her this for me…"

CHAPTER 14

*C*hloe was quite pleased with the way her plan was proceeding. Obviously she'd been right about Emily all along. The girl quickly got word to Hawk. The very next day she was to meet him in the grove in the very spot where he'd robbed her carriage, but she was to come alone, no carriage, no driver.

She realized it wasn't right to borrow things without asking, but she couldn't very well tell Lady Fiona what she intended. Choosing a mild-mannered mare, one that was older, rarely ridden and wouldn't likely be missed, she started out of the stables, but not before noting that Lord Lindale's bay was missing from its stall. However, that meant little for a man who was known to carouse the streets by night; he was rarely home at this hour.

Well, it was his life, she told herself. She wasn't any part of it—nor would she ever be. He'd used her for a purpose and then he'd cast her away when she was no longer useful. He'd kissed her, then thoroughly dismissed her.

But it was a good thing she wasn't some silly miss who aspired only to become someone's wife. She was too strong to be ruled by a husband—not that Lord Lindale wanted anything more than a dalliance.

Nor did it matter.

She wasn't in love with him.

In fact, she didn't even like him…

Not much.

The problem was—she frowned—she was no longer certain who he was or what he stood for. He'd managed to thoroughly confuse her.

The only person Chloe had ever truly been close to was her father and now he was gone. She'd loved her mother dearly, but her mother died when she was only eleven. Chloe had no one left in her life, except acquaintances, and that was perfectly fine with her. If one never allowed oneself to get close to someone, one couldn't be hurt once they were gone.

She didn't need anyone to make her happy. Her greatest joy in life was the good she could do for others. And to that end, there was no room in her life for a husband who would enslave her to his every wish. Her father always allowed her free rein. He had treated her more as a friend than a daughter. He had joyfully shared his vast wealth of knowledge, completely disregarding her gender. He had acknowledged her mind and her abilities, and for that, she was fortunate, indeed.

It was a good thing she never allowed her heart to falter.

The night was dark and once again presented a lowering fog, but Chloe was undaunted. She was more determined than ever to discover the truth about Hawk.

Upon reaching the grove, she tethered the horse and chose a tree limb to hang the kerchief that held the ring. She wasn't foolish enough to meet Hawk with the ring on her person, lest he decide to rob her yet again and keep the necklace and the ring, as well, but she fully intended to return it if he produced Fiona's necklace. To that end, she'd come early to prepare. After having secured the ring in a place where it wasn't visible, she hurried toward the road to wait, carrying a decoy kerchief in her hand.

It wasn't until she reached the road that Chloe began to feel a sense of unease. The night seemed to grow darker by the instant. And then, suddenly, he appeared as Emily had said he would, like the wind at her back. Though she hadn't heard him approach, he tapped her upon the shoulder.

Startled, Chloe spun to face him, her heart leaping into her throat. He'd come alone, as well. His men were either hiding in the woods nearby, or they hadn't accompanied him at all. Good. In truth, she could only deal with one thief at a time.

He eyed the kerchief in her hand.

Chloe smirked ever so slightly. She'd tethered the horse in a spot not far from the road, where he couldn't possibly have spied her hiding the ring. "It isn't polite to spy upon a lady," she admonished in an attempt to cover her fear.

"And so we meet again," he said, and bowed politely, ignoring her rebuke.

Chloe didn't return the courtesy.

She'd come to barter, not to trade pleasantries.

"I fully expected you to come with the constable," he confessed, and he cast a glance about to make certain they were, indeed, alone. He added, "My thanks to you for sparing me the task of having to dispose of the gentleman."

Chloe eyed him dubiously. Surely he hadn't meant that he would murder the constable? Still, she took a step backward. "Enough banter," she snapped with far more mettle than she felt. "This is not a tea party."

"Very well." He glanced once more at the kerchief.

"So I'm told you've something you wish to return to me?"

Chloe straightened, summoning her nerve, remembering the tales Emily told of the men he'd supposedly killed.

She shuddered and said a silent prayer that it was, in fact, Lord Lindale standing before her. If not, what might he do if he thought she'd crossed him? Her heart thumped like a hammer against her ribs. She longed to rip off his mask and expose him at last. She took a fortifying breath, lifting her chin defiantly, gathering her courage. "I would like to propose a trade," she said.

"A trade, madame?"

Chloe studied him. Indeed, he was the very same height as Lord Lindale and his voice seemed similar, as well—perhaps a wee bit deeper. She wished she could better see his eyes…and his mouth… "Indeed," she said, wavering in her convictions. "A trade."

"Let me guess," he said somewhat sardonically. "The ring for the necklace?"

Chloe nodded. "And something more."

"Something more?" he echoed, his tone sounding amused. He took a small step toward her.

Chloe nodded a little uncertainly.

BEAUTIFUL LITTLE VIXEN.

Merrick knew she was wary of him; he could see it in her gaze. And yet she stood there before him, making demands most men wouldn't dare impose.

She was brave coming here… alone.

"And what trade might this be?" he asked, sounding casual, feeling anything but. His body was taut, and his loins were afire merely at the sight of her.

She held out the bundle in her hand, teasing him with its presence. He hated to have to tell her that he

145

already had the deuced ring. He'd followed her and watched as she'd hidden it, knowing she was no imbecile. She wouldn't have stood before him with that ring in hand so that he could simply take it from her.

"The ring," she suggested coyly, "for the necklace… and your mask."

The deuced little shrew.

Merrick laughed softly. "And what is it you wish with my mask? Do you intend to join my merry band?"

"Of course not!" she exclaimed, sounding utterly appalled by the notion. But then, she seemed to reconsider it. She was clearly deluded if she thought he would allow it.

He asked her soberly, "What's to prevent me from simply taking the ring?"

"Go on, then," she taunted with a slight curve to her lips and a sparkle in her eyes. "Take it." She held out her hand a little farther, tempting him. "Do you think I am such a dolt I would simply hand a thief a ring?" She shook her head. "No, sir, I'm afraid the ring is hidden elsewhere."

"I see," Merrick said.

And he did; he saw far more than he dared.

Her breasts rose and fell with her breath and her nipples were taut against the bodice of her gown, taunting him with every breath she took. He eyed her pointedly. "I can't say I would bargain at that price. After all, I gave you the ring to begin with. What makes you think I wish it returned?"

She shrugged her shoulders. "You're here, are you not?" And she gave him a coy, little glance.

In that moment he wanted nothing more than to toss her over his shoulder like some crude barbarian and to carry her away to the cottage, only to have his way with her.

"What if I should propose my own little trade?" he

suggested, and for emphasis, he pulled the ring from his coat and showed it to her.

She gasped softly. "You followed me!"

"Of course I followed you," Merrick admitted without the least remorse. "What sort of thief would I be if I did not improvise?"

She scowled at him, clearly annoyed. "Well, you have the ring, so what is it you wish from me? Why are you still here?"

Merrick smiled shrewdly.

CHLOE GRIT HER TEETH, furious that he had outwitted her. But she should have known he would not deal fairly. He was a thief, after all!

"The necklace…"

Chloe blinked, disbelieving her ears. Surely he wouldn't simply return it to her.

"For a kiss."

Chloe's brows lifted. "That's all you wish from me? A kiss?"

"No," he replied. "But a kiss will do… for now."

Chloe's heart skipped a beat, but she dared to barter with him. "And what of the mask?"

"The mask remains upon my person," he declared, his tone unwavering.

It didn't matter.

With a kiss she would know all she needed to know. "And how can I be certain you will stop with only a kiss? You're a thief, after all," she told him. "Who is to say you'll not…"

"Ravage you?" he supplied with a grin.

Chloe nodded, her cheeks burning under his scrutiny.

"Because you have my word," he said simply.

Chloe arched a brow. "And what worth is there in the word of a known thief?"

"If you do not trust me... you may walk away," he suggested, but he withdrew the necklace from his pocket and dangled it teasingly before her, tempting her.

She considered his proposal, completely disarmed by the fact that he would give up so rich a prize for a simple kiss.

"Have you never heard of honor among thieves, flower?" he asked.

Chloe started at his endearment.

Flower.

He'd called her flower.

Lord Lindale had once called her the same.

It was him.

Emboldened by the knowledge, she told him, her heart beating faster, "But I am no thief, my lord."

He smiled behind his mask. And he didn't correct her when she used his title. "Ah, but you are. This we both know." He lifted up the ring and showed it to her, reminding her of her recent act of thievery.

Chloe chewed upon her lower lip as she eyed both the ring and the necklace, her belly fluttering wildly as she tried to determine what to do.

A simple kiss, she reasoned... for that alone he would return Lady Fiona's necklace.

What harm could come of it?

Her heart flipped against her ribs. "And you'll give me the necklace?" she asked, looking for reassurances.

He nodded once, positively. "After... that is—" he dangled the necklace before her "—if you can live with the knowledge that this necklace might have fed an entire village."

Chloe's brows drew together.

It wasn't fair that he should throw that at her. "It's a

148

matter of honor," she told him, and couldn't believe those words ever passed her own two lips.

For the longest instant their gazes locked.

MERRICK COULDN'T BELIEVE what he was about to say.

Merely a week ago he wouldn't have considered this perspective, but a vision of Rusty Broun's children came to mind, their gentle, dirty little faces appealing to his sense of compassion.

"And is your honor worth the life of a child?" Even as he asked, he decided, once and for all, that while honor was worth quite a lot, the price of any life was far too high.

Chloe opened her mouth to reply, then closed it again, clearly at a loss for words.

It seemed to him that they had both shared a revelation of sorts this week. He could tell by the look in her eyes that she no longer was entirely clear on the answer to that question, and with that epiphany there was a communion between them unlike any he'd ever experienced. His heartbeat quickened painfully.

"No," she answered at last, her voice soft, her eyes still locked with his own, and then she added, "Perhaps you should keep the necklace, after all."

"And the kiss?" he dared to ask, dropping the jewels into his coat pocket. His casual tone revealed not a trace of the dread he felt. "Shall I keep it, as well?"

For a moment, she didn't respond and then she slowly shook her head.

Merrick's breath caught as she took a step forward, offering herself into his embrace. "The kiss is yours, if you still desire it. A bargain is a bargain. It is my choice, after all, to leave you the necklace."

Merrick needn't any more encouragement. He

closed the distance between them, sweeping her into his arms.

CHLOE MOANED SOFTLY as he embraced her.

Unable to resist, she melted into his arms. Dearest Lord, she knew it was wrong to want him, but she did. She had been so very wrong… this kiss would, indeed, lead her heart astray.

She feared it had already gone astray.

His lips touched upon hers and she whimpered softly, eager for the taste and warmth of his mouth. His tongue swept over her trembling lips, tracing the part, coaxing ever so gently.

"Open for me, flower," he demanded, his voice hoarse.

Chloe complied at once, parting her lips with a soft, desperate gasp for air.

The sensation of his tongue entering her dazed her. The warmth of his body lit hers afire against the cool night air. She clung to him desperately, never wanting to let go.

He must have sensed the weakening of her limbs, because his arm tightened about her waist, drawing her fully against him so that she felt the hard lines of his very male form.

His tongue swept through her mouth, loving her with every stroke, tasting her, consuming her soul.

Chloe moaned softly and her body shuddered in secret places. Like a wanton, her breasts longed for the touch of his hand. Her body betrayed her, warring with her head.

She needed desperately to see his face.

Her hand curled over his shoulder, reveling in the width and breadth of him. Her heart racing, she gripped at his mask in an attempt to draw it up to expose him.

He caught her wrist, preventing her. "Not yet," he whispered against her mouth. "Not yet, Chloe."

Chloe shuddered softly at the intimate sound of her name upon his lips.

It didn't matter; she knew him by his taste.

Desperate for this union, she dared to return his hungry kiss, pushing her tongue timidly into his mouth, giving as he gave.

He groaned in response and she felt his body harden against her.

MERRICK'S BODY ignited with desire.

She was kissing him back with such abandon that it fueled his lust beyond reason. His blood burned through his veins like molten silver. Caught in a fierce storm of desire, he lifted her against him and carried her away from the road, deeper into the field, away from prying eyes. This very instant, his brain fogged with desire, he was no longer in command of his will. If she didn't stop him, if she didn't tell him no, he would take her... right here, right now... in the grass.

He lay her down, ravaging her mouth as they fell together.

God help him, he craved not only the taste of her lips, but the sweet nectar of her body. His hands caressed her hungrily. He wanted to taste her, wanted to bury himself inside her, to feel her secret places convulse with pleasure.

Chloe never wanted him to stop.

She was swept into a haze of passion, her body responding to his kisses with a fever of emotion. Never in her life had she felt this way about any man. Never had she longed for something more… to be kissed… to be held… to be loved.

She'd never realized how very empty she'd felt, until now…when the need to be filled was overwhelming.

"I am not who you think I am, Chloe," he said, his whisper hoarse as he rolled to one side of her. His hands set her skin aflame wherever they touched.

Chloe trembled. "I know," she whispered back.

It didn't matter.

Their lips met once more, their tongues entwining feverishly. His hands slipped beneath her gown, caressing her leg… first one… then the other… heat sliding upward to her most private regions. Chloe braced herself. Though she wanted him to take her, and she craved it, she had never been touched before.

Her body shuddered as his fingers slowly ascended, teasing her with their excruciatingly slow ascent.

"Please," she whimpered, though she hadn't the first clue what she was begging for.

MERRICK WAS CONSUMED in a rage of passion.

Blinded by desire, he ripped off the mask, wanting nothing at all between them. He tossed the mask aside.

Her skin was so soft… so lovely…

"God, you're so beautiful, Chloe," he whispered, and meant it from the depths of his soul. She was beautiful inside and out. He felt her tighten the muscles of her thighs and demanded, "Open for me, flower."

She did so, parting her thighs, and his loins throbbed violently, imagining the way it would feel inside her… like soft, deep warm velvet. When, at last, he touched her mons, his heart nearly burst through his chest. She was damp for him already. He closed his eyes and gently slid a finger inside, then stopped.

She was a virgin.

The knowledge sobered him.

They were in a field, in the cold damp night air. Anyone could come by and spy on them. His breathing labored, he removed his hand from beneath her skirt. This wasn't the way he wished her to remember her first time.

She stiffened. "What's wrong?"

Nothing was wrong.

Nothing at all.

His heart swelled with something like love. He wanted more for Chloe than for her to lose her virginity in the middle of a dirty field on a cold, damp night.

Still, he closed his eyes, craving the taste of her more than he craved his next breath. Lifting his finger to his lips, he slid the tip into his mouth, savoring the sweet nectar of her body. Christ, he'd not be deprived of this much.

"What's wrong?" she asked, her voice trembling.

He slid his hand through her hair, caressing her. "It's nothing, flower. Nothing at all... I simply don't wish to hurt you."

CHLOE'S HEART SANK.

The look on his face was so full of regret.

He might not want her for more than this, but he'd given her one thing, at least. He'd trusted her enough to remove his mask. Her hand moved to caress his face, feeling the contours of his face. Her heart pounded so loudly she knew he must hear it, as well.

And then she realized it wasn't her at all... there was a roar in the distance. The ground reverberated beneath them.

"Do you hear that?" he asked, his head lifting to the sound.

Chloe thought, at first, that it must be thunder, but then she recognized the sound.

Merrick realized it first, leaping to his feet, pulling her up quickly from the ground.

For an instant they stared at one another, panic-stricken, and then Chloe took him by the hand. "This way!" she demanded and dragged him behind her, stopping only long enough to seize his mask from the ground.

She pulled him toward the horse she had tethered. Protecting him was her first concern.

hloe and Merrick were no sooner settled together on the horse when the approaching riders came thundering to a halt before them. It was the constable and four of his men.

Merrick picked at something in her hair—weeds perhaps—and her face burned. She knew how it must appear. She could scarcely face Constable Tolly when he spoke.

"Good evening, Lindale," he said to Merrick. And then to her, "Evening, Miss Simon."

"Evening, Constable Tolly," Chloe replied, but she averted her face, too embarrassed to face him.

Her reputation would be irrevocably damaged after this; it was inevitable. It was all she had left of value and it wasn't as though she would have any recourse. She wasn't nobly born, and Ian wasn't required to make things right between them.

It didn't matter, she told herself. It was her decision and she would live with the consequences.

Chloe averted her gaze, staring blindly at the horse's mane.

. . .

As AWKWARD AS the moment was for Merrick, there was only one thing he regretted—the look on Chloe's face.

"Constable," he said in greeting.

The constable cleared his throat. "If you will, please forgive the lateness of the hour. I journeyed from Edinburgh as soon as I heard about Miss Simon's unfortunate incident." He studied Chloe carefully. "Are you quite all right, Miss Simon?"

Chloe lifted her chin, but wouldn't look at him. "Of course," she said. "Lord Lindale was…" She peered up at Merrick uncomfortably.

Merrick knew she hadn't any guile. She hadn't the first clue what to say. "We were… ah… returning from Rusty Broun's," he explained to the constable.

Chloe glanced back at him, something like surprise in her expression. He could tell her brain was quick at work putting pieces together. He certainly hoped he was right about her, because if he wasn't, he was putting more than himself and Ian at risk. He was putting Rusty at risk, as well.

"His little girl is ill," Merrick improvised, ignoring the look on Chloe's face. "Miss Simon was kind enough to attend the child."

The constable's brows rose.

Once again, he eyed Chloe and this time his eyes traversed the length of her, taking in her disheveled state, no doubt. "I should say it's quite the thing that you could take the time to accompany her, my lord. I'm certain you should feel honored, Miss Simon."

Chloe swallowed. He could hear it clearly. "Yes, of course," she said, her voice a bit shivery. She still couldn't face the constable. Her gaze remained steadfast upon the horse's mane. She reached out and lifted a coarse strand of horse hair, spinning it idly between her fingers.

Nothing escaped the constable's quick eye. Merrick knew the man noted everything, from the way she skirted his gaze, to the strands of grass that adorned her beautiful hair. He would have plucked them out for her, but he didn't wish to call any more attention to them than was already inevitable. He knew she'd made a tremendous sacrifice for his sake, and he fully intended to make this right for her.

She would not be ostracized, nor humiliated—not any more than she already felt this evening.

Merrick intended to make her his wife.

He didn't bloody care that she hadn't the bloodline his father was seeking. She was everything Merrick wanted. He couldn't give her Ian's name and he couldn't tell her the truth until he found the answers he sought.

"I suppose," the constable suggested, "I should pay Mr. Broun a visit. The poor man has borne more than his share of loss. Nothing serious, I hope?" he asked, looking directly at Chloe.

Chloe shook her head.

Good lass, Merrick thought. The less said the better.

Obviously, thinking to reach Rusty before Merrick could alert him, the constable said, "Well, then, I'm certain Miss Simon is weary after the evening's trials. If it suits you, my lord, I'll return first thing on the morrow."

"Of course," Merrick replied, unruffled by the veiled threat. He knew without a doubt that Rusty would cover for him, but the constable's incessant hounding shed a little light on one of the reasons Ian may have fled Glen Abbey. Aside from the fact that Ian likely sought his own answers, the constable evidently suspected something already. His brother was probably feeling the wall at his back.

Christ, but Merrick was beginning to feel it as well, and he'd done nothing at all.

The constable gave him a curt wave. "You have a good evening, my lord." But he said nothing to Chloe, merely gave her a disapproving glance, then left.

"Well," Chloe said, her head still down, "that was rather awkward."

"You've no need to worry, Chloe. Trust me, and everything will be fine."

Chloe nodded, but still wouldn't look at him.

He drew her closer to him, squeezing gently. "Do you trust me?" he asked.

She turned to look at him, then, and her eyes were glistening dark pools.

Merrick's heart twisted at the sight of her tears. He leaned forward to kiss them away.

"Trust me," he begged, and held her tightly as he spurred the mount away.

THE FOLLOWING MORNING, while Merrick saw the constable to his carriage, Fiona waited for her son to return to the drawing room. She shuddered over the risks he was taking—both with his own life and now with Chloe's.

She simply must find a way to make things right in this house, before everything fell to pieces.

She was furious at Ian for jeopardizing the reputation of a decent young lady. Of course, Fiona wanted them together, but she wanted it to be for all the right reasons. She'd sorely hoped Ian would see the things Fiona saw in Chloe. But, until now, her son was preoccupied with only one thing.

From a distance she'd watched Chloe grow from a child to a beautiful young woman. As a little girl, Chloe had been a solitary thing. Her father had kept her always by his side, tutoring her in the miracles of medicine. In this dwindling town, Chloe seemed to fit nowhere—much like Ian and for many of the same reasons. But Ian had snuck away like the mischievous boy to play with the tenant's children, all the while, Chloe had been ensconced in her little house.

Fiona sighed.

Truth be told, Ian was still playing with the tenant's children, she feared. And the game was much the same, save that the consequences were far more dire. And she hadn't the least notion why she and her son skirted the topic so vehemently when each of them knew very well what was at play.

Tapping her fingers impatiently upon her invalid chair as she awaited Ian's return, she determined that she was going to give her son a long overdue thrashing. She simply would not allow him to abuse Chloe's reputation—or her heart. Already, there had been enough heartache suffered in this house.

"Ian," she said when he walked into the drawing room. "Please close the door." She had never spoken to him so harshly, not even as a child, but everything was at risk now.

Everything.

He lifted his brows, giving her that same sardonic expression that reminded Fiona far too much of his damnable father, but he did as she bade him and sauntered into the room.

He fell back into the settee, looking weary, regarding her curiously.

"I must insist! You will wed Chloe at once!" she told him. And she meant it. "It was ungentlemanly of you to place her in such an imprudent position!" Among other veiled accusations, the constable claimed Chloe had been covered in weeds and that her hair and clothing had been mussed and dirty. While Tolly would keep his tongue over the matter, his men doubtless would not.

Merrick's brows lifted higher. "You're afraid for her reputation and yet you encouraged the evening at the cottage?"

"Yes, but a private meal together in a romantic mise en scène is hardly the same as a public roll in the meadow!"

She hated to be so vulgar about it, but it was what it was. "I did not bring Chloe into this house solely as my attendant. The truth is I felt obliged to bring her into my care. After all, she is the daughter of a longtime friend, and you may not feel any duty toward her, but I certainly do!"

He remained silent, listening intently.

Fiona reasoned with him. "There isn't much I request of you, Ian. We both know you travel your own path. But in this matter I will put my foot down. You will not abuse her."

He said nothing, merely looked at her, and placed a finger to his mouth as though he were considering her argument.

"Ian," she reasoned, softening her tone. "I realize how you feel about marrying until after you've inherited. But if you wait until then, it will be too late for Chloe. I beg of you to consider her well-being in this matter."

"So you want me to wed her... right now?" he repeated, sounding a little aghast at the notion.

Fiona straightened in her chair, cursing herself that she should be trapped by her own lies. God's bloody truth, she couldn't wait to get into the privacy of her own room so she could dance and run about like a madwoman.

"Yes, I do," she replied without hesitation, and tried to calm herself, knowing it would gain her little to push

Ian too far. He was strong-headed, like his father. "I know you feel frustrated by the fact that you've no control in this estate—as yet. I know you must feel an impostor with no land to accompany your title, but you *must* trust me. Someday everything will return to you."

Namely, once she was dead and Julian no longer felt the need to bind her to him. Fiona's heart squeezed painfully. Though she wouldn't be alive to see it, she dreaded the day Ian would discover the truth. And he would, she feared, because once she was gone, Julian had sworn to return Glen Abbey Manor to Ian. Once her son knew the truth, Ian would never forgive her, she knew—for denying him the truth about his father.

Merrick nodded, listening, his narrow-eyed expression somehow an accusation in itself. "And... in the meantime we must live on the meager earnings of poor folks who can scarcely afford to feed their young?"

Fiona frowned at him, hating the way the truth sounded.

"Where do the rest of the funds go, Mother?" he persisted. "Why do you not allow me access to the books? Why does Edward dole out paltry allowances?"

Fiona winced at his questions. "Why must we go through this again and again? Someday, Ian—though you'll not like what you discover—you will have complete control of this land and this house and you may do whatever you wish at that time. Give away the tenants' lands, have them all move into Glen Abbey Manor, do what you will... but until then, I only ask that you respect my wishes and my privacy."

Merrick listened intently, restraining the temper that was smoldering inside him like a combustible flame.

It was the first opportunity he'd had since arriving at Glen Abbey Manor to gain the answers he sought. He wasn't about to let the opportunity go. But the more he heard, the angrier it made him. Not only had his own life been a miserable pack of lies, but his brother had obviously lived like a pawn in his own home. It was no wonder Ian took matters into his own hands. It humbled him to hear the things his mother thought Ian might do with his inheritance. If, in truth, she believed those things, then Fiona was right about him. His brother was a good and decent man.

"In the meantime," he persisted, "Am I to remain the puppet master of this house?"

The woman who abandoned him had no answer to that question.

He pressed her. "Am I to allow the townsfolk to believe I am willing to drain them of their last coin only to satisfy the needs of this estate?"

"Ian," his mother said, her voice pleading.

He hadn't meant to make her cry, but her eyes grew misty. Still, she held her head up proudly, meeting his gaze. Merrick didn't know whether to feel pity or pride in her reaction. At the heart of the matter was this simple fact: He didn't know her at all. She hadn't allowed him that opportunity.

Why did she choose Ian over him?

Once again, a wave of envy came over him regarding the brother he didn't know. But it was ridiculous considering that Merrick grew up with the proverbial silver spoon in his mouth and his brother had obviously been tossed meager scraps from his table.

His father had long ago handed over the finances to Merrick, but Merrick never once saw a single reference to Glen Abbey in the ledgers. Whatever money the estate made through rents or investments did not go into the royal coffers, so the question remained... where did the funds go?

Not into the house, nor toward the care of its mistress, that much was certain. His mother's gown—as were all the gowns she'd worn in his presence—was quite modest. Unlike the royal palace in Meridian, the house had very few servants. And he knew for certain that Ian didn't have access to a single copper.

Which left only one possibility.

Merrick's nostrils flared with anger.

Edward.

Every time, it returned to Edward.

But how to prove it when he didn't have access to the books?

It was evident his mother was too afraid to stir the pot, lest Ian discover the truth. And, Merrick might loathe what Fiona had done but he believed she was a good woman—he could see it in her eyes and in the care she offered Chloe.

She started to weep in earnest, and she shook her head. Her hand covered trembling lips. "I cannot bear it that you will know my sins," she confessed, her tone full of heartbreak.

Merrick wanted to say he already knew her sins.

Now what he wanted to know was why she'd committed them.

I fear I have damaged the lives of many, but you must believe I deeply regret the course of my actions...

His father's written words came back to him suddenly. *I fear I have damaged... my actions...* Not we, or our.

Piece by piece, the puzzle was assembling before him. It was a hideous monstrosity that made him close his eyes in pain.

CHAPTER 16

*O*utside the door to the drawing room, Chloe paused before knocking. She hadn't meant to eavesdrop, but she'd heard her name and couldn't help herself. Hearing their discourse had somehow left her feeling emptier than she'd ever felt in her life. Even after her father's death she hadn't felt so utterly spent. She swallowed the knot that rose in her throat and turned from the door.

Her first thought was to leave this place. But no— where would she go?

Besides, it wasn't her way to run away from anything. Her father always told her that it was best to face the world with one's head held high and to carry on proudly through life's most bitter trials.

So what if Ian didn't wish to marry her.

She already knew that much.

That she had allowed her heart to soften was her own fault. Still, she couldn't regret what she'd done last night, because she'd done it, not out of blind love, but because Hawk had deserved her protection. Though it was difficult for her to reconcile what she thought she'd known about Lord Lindale and what she knew about Hawk, he was still the man she had so greatly ad-

164

mired. And now, he was even more a hero in her estimation, because it was evident that he risked himself completely for the sake of others.

She'd heard his grief over the treatment of their people, and it was palpable.

She made her way toward the garden, needing a breath of fresh air to clear her mind. Tears stung her eyes, but she refused them. She made her way along the pathway and sat upon a bench near Lady Fiona's rose garden.

Nothing had changed in her life, she assured herself. She was still the same person, with the same dreams. She had never really wanted a husband anyway.

Why should that suddenly change?

His kisses alone were not the source of her affection for him—nor was it the way he made her body feel. She had so long ago fallen in love with the heart of the man known by all as the infamous Hawk. Now that he had a face and a name, and she knew him for what he was, she could not turn her heart away from him.

He was, indeed, kind and compassionate. He was generous, noble and brave.

Chloe hadn't the first notion how long she sat there before she felt his presence, but suddenly he was there...

He sat quietly beside her on the bench.

"Good afternoon, my lord," she said stiffly, crossing her hands over her lap, hardening her heart against him.

He set his hand atop hers and the simple touch disarmed her at once. Tears pricked at her eyes. "No need for formalities between us, Chloe."

Chloe lifted her chin and tilted him a glance, willing away the flood of emotion that threatened to overcome her composure. "What, then, should I call you, my lord?"

He seemed genuinely perplexed by the question.

He merely sat there, staring at their combined hands piled carelessly atop her lap.

FOR A MOMENT MERRICK was unable to answer.

What should she call him, indeed.

He wasn't Ian and he couldn't reveal himself as Merrick. Nor did it please him for her to continue to call him my lord. He laughed quietly. "You seemed to have had plenty else to call me before now," he said lightly, teasing her. "Selfish, arrogant, spoiled," he suggested a few. "Shall I continue?"

She peered up at him and gave him a reluctant smile. "I no longer believe those things, my lord."

"Ah," he countered, "because suddenly I am beloved, kind, compassionate, generous, charitable, noble and brave," he said, repeating the things she'd once recited about Hawk.

She laughed softly and the sweet sound of it completely enchanted him. "You've a good recollection, my lord. Have you committed everything I've said to memory?"

"Yes," Merrick answered honestly, and he smiled at her. "I live for your every word, don't you realize?"

It was true.

He spent every waking moment that he wasn't with her recalling their conversations and musing over Chloe Simon's perspective of the world. She was witty and intelligent. She was beautiful and kind. Through her eyes, he had learned to see his brother for who he was and even to respect him. It was a gift he could never repay.

Chloe made him want to be a better man.

She lifted a delicate brow. "I rather doubt that," she said.

"But it is true," Merrick assured.

"My lord, you scarcely even spoke to me before a week ago."

Merrick squeezed her hand. "Then I was a fool," he told her, and he meant it. Whatever else Ian might be, he was certainly a fool if he had not seen the treasure sitting right beneath his very nose.

"Come," he said. "Let us walk apart." He tugged gently at her hand, dragging her to her feet.

"That's really not necessary."

"Yes, it is," he argued. "I wish to show you some-thing," he told her, his tone brooking no argument. He crooked her arm through his own and led her along the garden path toward the aviary.

"It seems you haven't been here much lately," Chloe commented as they entered the bird sanctuary.

In fact, Merrick had only seen it from a distance. Inside, it was well kept, he noted, but held very few birds—two gyrfalcons, a peregrine and an old saker. Like Merrick's, its color was almost white, a rarity for its breed. He went directly toward it and reached out to fondle the feathers. The falcon peered at his hand cu-riously.

"Sakers are the favored birds of Oriental and Arab falconers. Their hunting is far less hurried and impul-sive than other falcons, but when it finds what it wants, it goes after it with deadly precision."

Like the bird perched before him, it had taken Mer-rick a long, long time to find his heart, and now that he had, he wasn't going to let her go so easily.

"Really?" she said, her tone genuinely curious. She reached out tentatively to touch the bird and then changed her mind. "Have you always kept falcons?"

"Always," he replied, and it was the truth. He sus-pected Ian had, as well. "For a time, I would even sneak the bird into my room and perch it upon my bedpost."

He laughed softly at the memory. "The maids didn't like it very much," he admitted. "And it was overall not a very sanitary practice."

Chloe stifled a small laugh. He longed to make her laugh again, and to see that laughter reach her eyes. While she was feisty and full of life, one thing he hadn't recalled since meeting her was a true smile.

"I'm certain Edna had quite a lot to say about that," Chloe commented.

"Edna?" he asked.

"You don't remember her?"

Merrick shook his head.

"Has much of your memory returned?"

Merrick answered honestly, "I see more than I wish I saw. Tell me, Chloe... my mother and your father... they knew each other a long time?"

Chloe peered up at him, smiling. "Yes. In fact, my mother used to complain that my father spent more time wiping your nose than he did mine." She laughed softly. "Lady Fiona was... shall we say... a rather doting mother."

Disarmed by her disclosure, Merrick raked a hand over his face. She couldn't have known that his mother had never doted upon him a moment in her life—neither Fiona, nor the woman his father married.

"I believe she summoned my father every time you skinned your knee." A sparkle came into her eyes as she revealed, "I'm afraid my father thought you a mischievous little imp."

Merrick had to smile at that. Apparently it was something he and Ian had in common. Ryo had often rebuked him for the same.

"I must confess that I rather agreed," Chloe told him. "I only saw you in church, but you never behaved, and I didn't particularly like you," she confessed.

Merrick chuckled. "Not much has changed, I suppose."

They shared a meaningful look.

"I... no longer feel that way."

Merrick tested the bird's patience, reaching out to gently touch the falcon's head. It responded calmly, with but a quick fluttering of its wings. A small white feather floated to the ground. Merrick bent to retrieve it. He handed it to Chloe.

"Soft," she purred.

Like her skin, Merrick thought.

Warm velvet.

His body convulsed at the memory of her silky flesh beneath his fingertips, and he yearned to touch her again. God only knew, he wanted to touch her like that for the rest of his days.

He hoped Chloe would bear him sons and daughters. He wanted a houseful... a little brood like Rusty's that would swing on his coattails and wipe their dirty hands on his pant legs.

He bloody well didn't need Fiona to tell him to do the right thing by Chloe. He wanted to make things right by her.

He took her by the hand and turned to face her, hoping she would see the sincerity in his eyes. "Chloe," he began.

She averted her gaze, refusing to look at him, and snatched her hand away. "No, my lord! You needn't do that," she said, sounding utterly panicked. She turned then, and ran out of the aviary, leaving him to stare, dumbfounded, after her.

"Chloe!" he called after her, but she ignored him, hurrying toward the house, nearly tripping over her skirts in her haste.

Merrick wanted to follow, but perhaps it was best to let her go for now. He couldn't say the things he wished to and until he could... perhaps it was best to say nothing at all.

THOUGH SHE WAS FAR TOO preoccupied to participate in conversation, Lady Fiona's pleasant chatter helped keep Ian off her mind while Chloe massaged her limbs.

Chloe hadn't meant to flee like some silly miss; she simply couldn't have borne anything Ian might have to say.

If, in fact, he were to ask her to wed him, she would know it wasn't by his desire and she would have denied him. It would have broken her heart. On the other hand, "goodbye" would have been equally as excruciating.

Fiona's color seemed far healthier than it had been merely a week ago, she thought, and on impulse, she gave the arch of the foot a gentle pat.

Her foot twitched.

Chloe blinked, at first, disbelieving her eyes. But, indeed, it had responded, she was certain of it.

She met Lady Fiona's gaze in surprise. The two stared at one another—Chloe's eyes questioning and Lady Fiona's perfectly blank. But something about her expression—or lack of it—gave Chloe pause. It seemed to Chloe that Lady Fiona knew what happened and yet she sat there, saying nothing about her miraculous recovery. In fact, it rather seemed to Chloe that she was attempting to ignore the phenomenon altogether. "Did you feel that?" Chloe asked, thinking she would surely acknowledge it.

Lady Fiona smiled serenely and asked, "Feel what, my dear?"

Chloe drew her brows together, confused by Fiona's

reaction. "I thought I saw something, but perhaps I was mistaken."

Lady Fiona sat upright in the bed, her legs stretched before her, looking completely unruffled by the incident.

Chloe's old suspicions reared. Contemplating the odd reaction, she pulled the coverlet up over Lady Fiona's legs, pursing her lips as she considered the possibilities.

"You're doing such a great job, my dear," Lady Fiona said gently, praising her but completely disregarding what had only just transpired.

Chloe frowned. "Thank you."

Was Lady Fiona faking her injury?

Why would she lie?

Each day, this house seemed to unveil yet another secret. Everyone here seemed to have them: Lady Fiona, Ian, even Edward. For a week now the cranky steward had locked himself away in his office. He'd taken his meals there and slept there, as well. Whatever could he be up to?

One thing was certain: whatever it was, it was evident that he had Lady Fiona's blessing, because she was the one who'd requested his meals be delivered.

As for Ian, he'd journeyed to Edinburgh—to sell the necklace no doubt—and had yet to return. Chloe was glad he was gone because it pained her too much to see him.

Tucking the coverlet gently about Lady Fiona's waist, she said a brief good-night. Unfortunately, she left without putting out the light and didn't recall it until nearly an hour later. Chloe returned to Lady Fiona's room, feeling miserable over the fact and hoping the light from the candle hadn't disturbed Fiona's slumber. She knocked softly on the door.

There was no answer.

Frowning, Chloe knocked again, a little harder this time.

When there was still no response, she peered beneath the door. No light seeped beneath. Her candle was out. How strange. Lady Fiona was evidently a heavier sleeper than Chloe realized.

That... or she wasn't in her room at all.

DRESSED IN A MODEST NIGHTGOWN, Fiona stood, looking over Edward's shoulder, watching as he removed entries from the ledger that sat on his desk. Edward was the only person in the house who knew the truth about her condition. Unfortunately, he knew about Ian's misadventures, as well. Still, Fiona trusted him to keep silent. Whatever else he might be, Edward was also Julian's agent. She knew he would never dare betray her confidences, lest he experience Julian's wrath.

"I don't want Ian to ever know where it goes," she instructed him. "If he sees how much money is funneled into that account, he will wonder why."

"Yes, madame."

It pained her to know that Ian took such risks when money was available to him—if only Julian chose to release it. "If Julian wishes to reveal himself once I am gone, he may do so, but I cannot bear the thought of ever facing my son were he to discover all the hideous lies."

"Yes, madame."

"I am heartily ashamed," Fiona assured him. And she was. She should have done something long ago, but what could she have done? She wanted desperately to be able to give Ian something after she was gone. If she kept her mouth shut, he would have a future with Glen

Abbey Manor. If she didn't, he would have nothing at all, and neither would she. Ian would surely disown her, and Julian would carry out his threat and seize the manor and everything attached to it.

He'd lied to her all those years ago.

She may not have ever left Merrick had she realized Julian would renege upon his word. She would have remained in Meridian with both of her sons and said nothing to risk being driven away.

"Yes, madame."

As she studied the ledger, a particular entry caught her attention. She pointed at it, tapping her finger gently upon the open book. "What is that one, Edward?"

Edward straightened. He cleared his throat. "That would be... let's see... miscellaneous expenditures, madame."

Fiona screwed her face at his explanation. "Miscellaneous expenditures? I don't understand." She squinted to better see the line in question. It was an extraordinary sum. She narrowed her eyes to it. "I thought Julian expected a detailed inventory of all our expenses?"

"Yes, madame, his royal highness does, indeed, expect a detailed report." His face mottled under her scrutiny. "But these were funds that my lord requested, and he would not give me a reason for their appropriation."

"Julian?"

"No, madame. Master Ian."

"Ian?" Fiona asked, with no small measure of surprise. "You gave these funds to Ian? But he complains incessantly that you will not open the bank for him at all."

Fiona scanned the rest of the ledger with a shaky finger and found another marked miscellaneous.

"Good Lord! I cannot even imagine what he would use that sort of money for!" She cast Edward a glance. The steward merely looked up at her, his face red, but his expression cast in stone.

"How long ago was this?" She glanced at the date—two months past. "Has Julian not taken us to task over it yet? I cannot believe he has not cut off our funds entirely. Let me see that ledger!" she commanded, seizing it before he could hand it over. "Where are the rest of the books, Edward? I should pore over these myself. I've not done so in far too long. Give me everything, please, both the ledgers you have doctored and those left untouched."

Edward suddenly looked horrified. "But, madame! There are too many to go over tonight."

She eyed him dubiously but relented. "I suppose you are right." She glanced at the timepiece he had sitting upon the desk. "And the hour grows later. I should hie to bed.

"Please do not touch the rest of these books, Edward," she directed. "I wish to look through them before they are altered any further."

"Yes, madame," he said, his tone stiffer than it had been. "I'll have them ready and awaiting you on the morrow."

"See that they are," Fiona said curtly. As she left him, she pursed her lips while she considered the ledgers.

Something didn't quite add up.

CHAPTER 17

*W*hat was the significance of that ruby ring? Chloe lay abed, unable to sleep, her head spinning with questions. The hour was growing so late that she feared morning would come before she could chance to close her eyes.

Where was Ian?

Wherever he was, she hoped he wasn't in danger. She had a terrible feeling that the constable was watching his every move. But she wondered how the constable knew to suspect Ian. Chloe certainly never would have. He'd played the part of a dandyish lord so well that she doubted anyone suspected him.

Did Lady Fiona know her son was a champion to the poor? His mother had claimed it was Hawk who'd caused her carriage accident. But that couldn't be... unless... her story was fabricated.

And then a thought occurred to her: Had she, like Chloe, used the accident in an attempt to draw him out?

She recalled that Ian had forced his mother, against her will, to make a report to the constable. They'd summoned Chloe's father first, of course, but the constable came soon thereafter.

TANYA ANNE CROSBY

And the necklace... who filed that report with the constable? Certainly not Chloe. Although Ian said he would do so, he had not to the best of Chloe's knowledge—nor had Lady Fiona encouraged it.

Someone had to have also alerted the constable that she was to meet with Hawk that night. Chloe was sure of it. But who would have done so?

Emily?

So many questions nagged at Chloe's brain. Sleep seemed an impossible task. Footsteps wandered past her door and she wondered, in her sleep-deprived state, if it could be Lady Fiona wandering the halls. But as soon as she thought it, she admonished herself for the ridiculous notion. She couldn't believe Lady Fiona would lie about her illness.

And Chloe's father, he wasn't the sort to lie at all.

Remembering the weeks before he'd died, tears pricked at her eyes and she swallowed the knot that rose in her throat. He'd been quite beside himself for some reason Chloe could never determine. Had he lied for Lady Fiona? Had the ordeal sent him to an early grave?

Chloe couldn't bear it if that were true.

The echo of footsteps halted outside her door. Chloe peered up to see the shadow of feet paused outside. And then the hall light went out and the shadow blended into the darkness.

Her heart began to pound.

It wasn't her imagination; someone was outside her door.

The footsteps began anew, moving away from her door. They faded somewhere down the hall. Chloe heard a door creak open and close and she sucked in breath she hadn't realized she'd held. She lay her head back down upon the pillow, willing her heartbeat to slow.

Lord, she was beginning to see conspiracies in every corner—secrets and lies. And if there was one thing she couldn't abide it was a liar. Perhaps she shouldn't remain in this house any longer. Perhaps it was time to go.

She turned her back to the door to face the balcony, starting as she spied a figure standing there as well, the form a silhouette against the moonlight. Chloe froze, a scream caught in the back of her throat.

"Chloe," he whispered, and came toward the bed.

Chloe's heart flipped against her ribs at the sound of his voice.

"FORGIVE ME," Merrick said as he came to her bedside, looking down upon her.

He'd been gone a week and, God help him, he could think of nothing but Chloe. He couldn't stay away. He needed to know the feel of her body beneath his. He craved the taste of her upon his lips and his tongue. He wanted to know her body intimately, inside and out.

"Ian," she whispered.

The sound of his brother's name upon her lips burned at his gut. He wasn't Ian and he damned well wanted her to know it. She said nothing to protest his presence and his heart quickened its beat, thrumming through his veins. Illuminated by the pale moonlight, she was a vision of loveliness lying before him. But her face was in the shadow of his body and he couldn't see her expression. Her white, filmy nightgown clearly revealed the outline of her areolas, beautiful peaks that whetted his hunger.

"You're back," she said, her voice trembling slightly.

Merrick bent to kiss her, his lips unerringly finding her mouth. Eager for the feel of her, he growled softly in the back of his throat as she reached out to take him into her arms, willingly inviting him into her bed.

Tonight, he would make her his own.

He couldn't wait any longer.

His hand cupped her face as he deepened the kiss and her arms went sweetly about his neck, drawing him near.

Merrick didn't need further encouragement. He fell atop her, savoring the sweet taste of her mouth. "Chloe," he rasped, and was nearly unmanned on the spot when she offered him her sweet tongue. Fire pumped through his veins, increasing his size, making him throb painfully.

He kissed her feverishly, tasting and plundering the depths of her mouth, praying she'd not change her mind and send him away. If she did, he would surely die.

He'd been able to think of nothing more on the journey home from Edinburgh than burying himself into the silky depths of her body.

He wanted her body and soul.

His hands released her face long enough to untie his cravat. He tossed it impatiently to the floor, moaning softly as her hands gently cupped his face.

"I'm so glad you are here," she whispered, and his heart swelled against his ribs until it ached.

He tore off his coat, wrenching free of it, and tossing it to the floor, then his shirt, needing to feel the warmth of her skin against his bare flesh.

CHLOE SWALLOWED.

She wanted this.

She didn't care about tomorrow.

All that mattered was tonight, this instant.

If she must leave him tomorrow, then at least she

would take this moment with her and cherish it always in her heart. Tonight she would give him more than her love, she would give him her body... she would give him anything he desired and more.

Her hand slid from his face, reveling in the soft growth of whiskers there, and moved to his wide, beautiful shoulders, adoring his sinewy male flesh. His hands came to her once more, alighting first upon her shoulders and sliding down her arms, caressing feverishly. They were like fire against her body and yet she shivered wherever they lit.

Moaning softly, arching her back, Chloe willed him to take whatever he wished. Her head fell backward as he broke their kiss and his mouth moved down her chin, her throat, leaving little fiery kisses along its path.

She trembled as he gently suckled her throat, sending pinpoints of pleasure throughout her entire body.

Suckling through her gown, his mouth fell upon her breasts and she gasped for air, shuddering softly over the glorious sensations his suckling evoked. Scandalously, even through the material of her nightgown, she could feel the swirl of his tongue as it made tiny circles about her aching nipples. He found and traced the outline of her areolas and then drew first one peak, then the other into his mouth, suckling like a babe at its mother's breast.

It was wickedly sweet.

She had never known a man would wish to suckle that way. The sensation was unlike anything Chloe had ever known. She arched her body, wanting more. In answer, his hands moved beneath her, lifting her higher for the shockingly erotic feast, and something began to coil deep inside her. Tightening in her womb, the feeling intensified with every nip and suckle.

"I need you," he whispered.

Chloe's breath escaped in a rush.

She needed him, too.

Unable to speak, she nodded her assent. His body fell fully atop her then, and she reveled in his weight. Partly in fear and partly in delight, she whimpered as he covered her.

SO SWEET.

Merrick craved the taste of her lust. His hands gripped the front of her gown and ripped it.

He would buy her new ones.

He would buy her thousands of new gowns.

He would give her anything her heart desired.

She cried out, startled, but her face showed no trace of fear, only sweet passion. It filled him with intense satisfaction. The sight that greeted his hungry gaze literally stole his breath. Her breasts, revealed by the soft moonlight, were perfectly shaped for his hands, the nipples pebbled tightly, waiting like tiny rosebuds for his tongue's caress.

Christ, but she was lovely.

His mouth fell once more upon her breasts with a thirst unlike anything he'd known. He tasted her skin with abandon, lapping her gently, committing every small nuance of her body to his memory. She arched further, giving him greater access to her beautiful breasts, moaning softly, and his loins hardened at the feast she offered so willingly.

"I want you, Chloe," he whispered.

For a lifetime.

Forever.

Someday he wanted to die in her arms... after they had loved each other for a hundred years.

He reached down and took her by the hand, drawing her lean, delicate fingers to his manhood. He wanted her to feel what he would give her. He wanted her to grow accustomed to the thought of having him inside her. He wanted her to touch him, caress him, love him. He wanted her body to prepare for his possession.

And he would possess her.

CHLOE MOANED SOFTLY at the shocking feel of him against her trembling fingers. He was so big, so hard. She knew what he wanted and, Lord, she would give it to him freely.

Her body shivering, her fingers gripped him where he longed for her to touch him. His fingers closed about her own, forcing her to acknowledge the length and width of him. She whimpered deep in the back of her throat as his hand left hers to unfasten his trousers, and somehow, he shed them without displacing her hands. Or perhaps Chloe simply wasn't aware of it and her fingers sought him again in a haze of passion.

He made some tortured sound as her fingers gently closed about his shaft, gripping him awkwardly but eagerly.

He was beautiful, his body lean, but thickly muscled. His golden hair gleamed in the moonlight. His face, as he looked down upon her, was so full of desire that it sent shivers of delight through her.

While she stroked him, his mouth moved slowly down the length of her body, his hands ripping her gown as it descended toward her most private place and Chloe began to tremble in earnest, afraid he would continue... afraid he would stop. His manhood slid from her hand as he moved down her body, revealing droplets of desire at the tip. She felt the steely length of it glide, hard and demanding, down her thigh as he kissed first her belly and then her mons. The sensation of his mouth there gave her a start, dizzying her. She cried out at the sweet, sinful intimacy of the kiss as his tongue made gentle swirling motions about the bud of her womanhood, teasing and tasting.

The coil of pleasure tightened throughout her body, making her crave something more...

His hands joined his mouth, probing gently, his thumb stroking the part of her forbidden lips. His tongue swept inside her body, shocking her with the warm, wet caress. Chloe cried out in pleasure, arching her body in wicked delight.

"This is like a precious flower," he told her, parting her gently with his fingertips. His tongue lapped her hungrily as he spoke. "It has the sweetest nectar," he whispered.

Chloe's heart leaped into her throat.

His fingers continued to caress as his tongue tasted her feverishly. All the while, Chloe was drowning in a sea of her own desire. Of their own will, her legs spread for him, wanting to feel more.

"That's it, flower," he said, coaxing. "Open for me." And he drank from her like a hummingbird would a honeysuckle. He suckled and lapped her alternately. His fingers slid inside her body unexpectedly and the feel of it sent a violent shudder through her. He pushed deeper. Whatever pain she might have felt was eased by the delicate lapping of his tongue. Chloe was out of her mind with desire.

He was playing her body like an instrument, bringing her to higher and higher pleasures.

She was vaguely aware that her legs spread wider for him, scandalously allowing him to feast upon her in a way she hadn't even known a man would long to do. She'd understood very well how men and women coupled, but this... this was like nothing she had ever imagined.

SEDUCED BY A PRINCE

It was wicked and sweet, deliciously sinful.

As his finger pushed deeper inside her body she felt a sharp, quick pain and cried out.

He ceased his loving abruptly. "Do you want me to stop?" he asked.

Chloe shook her head frantically, unable to speak. In answer, her hands went to the back of his head, pulling him closer in desperation. She arched for him, wrapping her legs about his neck, wanting yet more of what he would give.

"Oh, God," Merrick groaned.

He willed himself to slow, wanting her first time to be pleasurable. His mouth sought her once more, his tongue parting the petals of her womanhood. Chloe whimpered and he deepened the kiss, reveling in her passion.

She was more than he'd imagined.

CHAPTER 18

"*D*o you trust me, Chloe?" Merrick asked.
She did.

Chloe nodded, trusting him completely.

His finger slid deeper within her body and she lifted her hips to accept it, delighting in the feel of it.

But she wanted more.

His breath sounding labored, he slid back up the length of her body, taking possession of her mouth again, suckling her lips, nibbling gently. Chloe tried to kiss him back, uncertain how to respond, not knowing how even to touch him to return the sensations. But she vowed to try. Her hands gripped at his shoulders, caressing. Her mouth kissed his salty flesh, lapping timidly.

And then she felt it… the pressure of his manhood begging entrance to her body, and she shuddered violently, knowing that once she gave this to him it would never be hers again to give. Even so… she wanted this more than she wanted to breathe.

Begging with her body, she undulated beneath him, coaxing him inside. He answered with a low moan deep in the back of his throat and she smiled to herself, hoping that it felt as wonderful for him as it did for her. He glided into the depths of her with excruciating slowness. Chloe cried out in pleasure, not in pain, as his shaft filled her completely.

Dearest God... this... this was Heaven. This... was like nothing she'd ever experienced before.

She wanted it never to end.

"You feel so good," he whispered against her cheek, and he began to rock gently against her, stroking her inside until she thought it would drive her mad.

MERRICK WAS beside himself with joy.

It might be his body filling hers, but she filled up his heart and his soul. Gently he placed his hands beneath her bottom and rocked himself inside her, controlling his thrusts as he pushed slowly deeper. He lengthened his stroke, his body trembling in anticipation of giving her his seed.

"I love you," he said, and meant it.

"I love you," she whispered, in the heat of passion, and his heart squeezed painfully.

She didn't know him.

How could she love him?

She simply hadn't realized yet that everything about him was a bloody lie. Still, he reveled in her words, vowing to make it up to her. But hearing her whisper those three little words sent him into a fog of passion. He thrust into her once more, his mouth catching and devouring her soft whimper of surprise. When her legs instinctively entwined about his waist, he was entirely lost. In that instant, even if he'd wanted to, he couldn't have stopped; he thrust again and again and again...

. . .

"YES," she said. "Oh, yes!" Chloe never wanted the moment to end. For the rest of her life she wanted to feel lost in his loving, safe in his arms.

She met his every thrust with one of her own, praying that she was giving him as much pleasure as he was giving her. Pleasure coiled like a snake through her body... building a sensation she needed desperately to explore. She closed her eyes and followed it to some place she'd never dared go. She sought it with every undulation of her hips, every gasping breath, and when, at last, her body convulsed around him, she cried out in absolute joy.

With a final violent thrust, he spilled himself inside her. His cries of pleasure gave Chloe a sense of completion such as she'd never understood until this very instant.

When it was over, they lay holding one another, neither able to speak. They fell asleep basking in the afterglow of their loving.

It was Merrick who awoke at first light, knowing he couldn't remain lest he bring her greater scandal. But he didn't wish to leave without loving her once more. He needed to feel her body wrapped about him again, gripping him like velvet steel.

He kissed her throat, her mouth...

She stirred awake and he settled his arm about her waist, pulling her atop his chest, so that she lay sleepily with her head atop his shoulder. She peered up at him groggily and smiled. Merrick thought it was the most beautiful smile he had ever witnessed.

"Good morning," she murmured, and tried to rise.

He stilled her with a hand to her back and she settled atop him, sighing softly.

"Good morning, flower," he said, and grinned at her, shifting her weight atop him so that his throbbing shaft was poised at the entrance of her body. He heard her soft gasp, but her hands merely wrapped about his neck in answer.

Closing his eyes, Merrick thrust upward, entering her in one swift motion.

He loved her until he could bear it no longer, stroking her from within. She cried out softly, panting, and he felt her begin to convulse about him and with a last surge he brought them both to completion. He held her a long moment, then rolled her from atop him, lying her gently upon her back. He rose from the bed, kissing her thoroughly.

CHLOE SIGHED, perfectly content.

Never in her life had she felt such incredible joy... such adoration for another human being.

As she lay there, basking in the light of Ian's gaze, she hoped he would look at her this way always. Never had she felt such a connection to another soul.

Gloriously naked, he fumbled with his clothing, dressing before her, watching her the entire time he dressed. Unashamed, Chloe watched him back, in silence, afraid to ruin the moment. She knew he must go, but she didn't want him to.

He withdrew something from his coat before putting it on. It was the ring he'd asked her to give to his mother.

He sat upon the bed and looked at her soberly. "Chloe, this is yours," he said, kissing her tenderly upon the forehead. He whispered, "Until I can make it right." He laid it down upon the pillow beside her.

Once he was gone, she felt his absence like a terrible void. For the longest time she could only lay there, contemplating the night's consequences. She was no longer a virgin, but she didn't care. She had long adored his heart. Now she loved his body and mind. There could be no one else for her.

Ever.

Studying the ring he'd left upon the pillow, she wondered whose crest it bore. It wasn't the MacEwen coat of arms, she knew. Their crest, wrapped with a ribbon of tartan, adorned the drawing room for all to see.

She considered briefly whether she should show it to Lady Fiona, and decided not to. At least until she understood its significance, it was best to keep it to herself.

Ian had asked her to trust him and she would.

She trusted him with her life.

FIONA DIDN'T EMERGE from her room all day long.

With the door closed, she sat upon her bed with the account ledgers piled on every side of her and on the floor surrounding the bed. After Edward delivered the bookkeeping that morning, she'd given him orders that not even Chloe should disturb her.

To her dismay, she'd yet to come across one book that wasn't curiously altered. Edward had either worked furiously and finished the majority of the changes before she'd asked him to stop, or he'd blatantly disobeyed her and continued to adjust them even after she'd asked him to stop.

But why would he do that unless he had something to hide?

The thought left her ill at ease. She had trusted Edward implicitly, not only with the household ledgers, but with far more information than she should have.

There was nothing in any of the books that was

even remotely similar to the entries she'd found in the one she'd discovered in his office, but, still, something didn't seem right about them. They had been altered in the manner she'd requested, but he'd given them to her all out of order and it was difficult to study them randomly. She began to organize the ledgers according to date—no easy task since they represented nearly thirty years of accounting. It took her the majority of day to assemble the piles by year. In the end, the piles were not even, though each pile should reflect the number of months in a year. Some piles contained merely six books, others eight.

There were a lot of books still missing.

Hoping to get to the bottom of it all, Fiona got into bed, settled herself so that it wouldn't appear she'd been up and about, then rang for Edward to come.

He was quick to arrive, rapping sharply at the door.

"Come in," Fiona commanded.

He did as she bade him and came inside, closing the door behind him. "Yes, madame?"

Fiona frowned at him. "Edward," she said, uncertain what, precisely, to say. She didn't wish to accuse him unjustly. "There seems to be a few ledgers missing."

He peered about the room, noting the twenty-seven neat piles and asked, "Missing, madame?"

"Yes." She slipped out of the bed, determined to show him what she'd found. "Look... eighteen twenty, eighteen twenty-three, twenty-four and twenty-five all have piles of merely six." She was speaking of the year of their creation. "Eighteen twenty-eight and twenty-nine both have only eight—June and November are missing. And eighteen twenty-nine and thirty are both missing February, June and November!"

Edward stared at the uneven piles, his expression perfectly blank. It gave her pause.

"Well... I must have simply overlooked the others,"

he said at last. "There were so many, madame." His expression seemed suddenly wounded. "You did not think I would keep them from you, did you?"

"Well, of course not!" Fiona felt instantly chagrined for having suspected him. "Yes, of course you overlooked them." she declared. Whatever had she been thinking? "Please have them delivered to me straightaway," she directed, lifting one of the books to pore over while she waited. It had been far, far too long since she'd involved herself with the household finances. It had always depressed her to know how little control she'd had over her own estate—and more, how little she was able to give her son. And therefore, she'd eschewed the task completely, leaving it to Edward's capable hands. After all, it was Julian he had to answer to, and she knew he wouldn't dare cheat his royal highness.

"Yes, madame," he said, leaving her again to peruse the ledgers she had.

CHLOE SIGHED as she peered out from the carriage, trying not to think of Ian.

With tears in her eyes, Aggie had begged her to come and tend her youngest sister. The girl had gotten a pin in her leg whilst scrubbing the parish floor. Poor Isabel was only eight years old and, like Aggie, was forced to take on hard labor to help feed her family. Whenever Chloe bemoaned her own circumstances, she needed only look to those unfortunate souls like Emily, Aggie and little Isa.

She smiled privately, thinking of Ian, who risked so much to bring a mere morsel of food to these good people's plates.

"You're thinking of my lord, are ye not, Miss Chloe?" Aggie said, gazing at her expectantly.

Chloe nodded, her cheeks burning a little hotter.

Was she so transparent?

"I knew it!" the girl exclaimed, her tone clearly pleased. "He's perfectly dreamy," she said, and sighed, as well.

Chloe couldn't bring herself to feel the least bit jealous over the look of adoration evident on Aggie's face. Every woman she knew felt the same way about both Lord Lindale and Hawk. But only Chloe knew that they were one and the same.

"Thank you for coming," Aggie said, peering out from the window as they rode into the town limits. She sat in the facing seat, her expression one of wonder since they'd departed Glen Abbey Manor. She was clearly unaccustomed to the luxuries of a coach, because she kept touching the carriage walls, feeling the velvety lining, running her hands over the plush leather seats.

"I assure you, it is my pleasure," Chloe said, and meant it truly. It wasn't as though Lady Fiona needed her anyway. In fact, she'd all but refused Chloe's attendance this morn.

Aggie peered up at her then, her expression suddenly regretful. "I don't know how I'll ever repay you, Miss Chloe."

"Nonsense," Chloe replied. "You did me a great favor, Aggie, now I shall do one for you."

"Thank you," Aggie said sincerely. "It's little wonder everyone loves you! You're so beautiful, smart and kind!"

Chloe blinked in surprise.

Aggie's disclosure took her aback. She hadn't realized anyone thought anything of her at all. She had, for most of her life, felt quite invisible, except to her father —not that she had been lonely. She hadn't had time to feel sorry for herself.

Aggie's expression turned to one of concern. "Isabel's been in terrible pain these last three weeks," she disclosed, worrying her lip. "She keeps a horrible fever and her leg stiffens so she cannot walk."

Chloe shook her head, not liking the sound of it. She was careful how she phrased her rebuke, lest Aggie feel responsible. "You must never again wait so long to come to me, Aggie, and you must never worry about payment. Promise me you will not."

Aggie nodded, preoccupied, and again peered out the window. "That's curious," she said suddenly, changing the subject yet again. "People are dancing in the street."

"Dancing?"

Chloe peered out the window and was startled to see so much revelry going on. There were people everywhere, dancing and shouting.

"That is, indeed, quite curious," she agreed.

Usually empty, the streets were filled with revelers —children running about their mother's skirts— women carrying baskets of goods.

"Oh, my! Look how many people are coming from Mr. Duncan's store!" Aggie exclaimed.

As they passed the general store, Chloe saw the shop owner put up a sign, bearing a happy grin on his face. She rapped sharply upon the carriage roof and the carriage came to an abrupt halt. She and Aggie fought to exit first, so curious were they. Both women spilled into the street, righting their skirts. Chloe, with Aggie at her heels, hurried to Mr. Duncan's store before he could close the door.

"There's nothing left!" he said cheerily before Chloe could open her mouth to speak.

"What do you mean, nothing left?"

He cackled happily. "Precisely what I said, Miss Chloe—nothing left on the shelves!"

"What has happened here?" Aggie asked a little girl who passed by. It was Rusty's daughter, chasing after her mother, who was so beside herself with glee that she scarcely noticed that one of her three daughters was struggling to keep up with her hurried pace.

The little girl lifted up her new doll. "It's Christmastime!" she declared.

Chloe shook her head, completely bewildered by the strange event they'd encountered. She stopped another woman who passed, her skirts filled with staples from the market.

"What happened here?" she asked the woman.

The woman smiled. "Havena' ye heard?"

Chloe shook her head.

"We're all rich!" she declared. "Hawk left us all baskets full of money—everyone, everyone!" she said joyfully.

"Everyone?" Chloe asked, aghast.

"Aye!" the woman said, and laughed again. "Oops!" she said, struggling to keep the bundle of goods neatly tucked in her skirt.

It was the necklace, Chloe realized, and tears stung her eyes. "When did he come?" she asked the old woman.

"Last night," she said, giggling beside herself. "He came like a thief in the night, bearing money and gifts for one and all."

Good lord! He must have done it all before he'd come to her and he'd never said a word about it. The realization humbled Chloe to her soul. He hadn't wanted praise, nor had he cared that she knew his good deeds. The knowledge tugged at her heart and thickened her throat.

The laughter and joy surrounding her were contagious. Chloe laughed, too. So did Aggie.

"I wonder what he left us!" Aggie said, excited. They raced back to the carriage, both eager to see what gifts had been left at Aggie's house.

CHAPTER 19

*W*hatever gifts had been left for Aggie's family, joy over it was tempered by Isabel's condition. Her leg infection was horrid, but thankfully not so bad that the leg couldn't be saved. Chloe had seen drawings and read many accounts of patients who'd lost their entire limbs over this wasting disease. Her father told her horrible tales of having to saw off arms and legs. It was a dangerous illness.

She found Isabel in her bed, sweating profusely, but her mood was barely dampened by her pain, because in her hand, she held a brand-new doll. Her elder brother sat upon the edge of her bed, recounting tales of what he'd encountered on the street.

Chloe's heart went out to them. They were troopers, every one. Aggie's mother died giving birth to Isabel. Her father died three years before. It was only the children in the household now—five of them in all—and they relied upon each other. Isabel was, by far, the youngest, with Jack, her cheery little guardian, being the next oldest by two years. The two were chattering feverishly while sweat beaded like dew after a storm on Isabel's brow.

Chloe was thankful she'd brought her father's bag,

which contained enough laudanum to put the girl to sleep while she operated. She sent the brother from the room, allowing only Aggie to remain to assist her. Their first task was to sterilize the bed and wound. They changed the bedding, then cleaned the wound with scalding water after Isabel was asleep and then Chloe surgically removed the infected tissue, praying it hadn't spread so much that she would have to amputate, after all. In the end, they were fortunate. It was a relatively mild case, and Chloe gave Aggie careful instructions on how to keep the wound sterile to prevent the infection from spreading. And though it wasn't her place to do so, she suggested Aggie stay with her sister to look after her, fully intending to take responsibility with Lady Fiona once she returned to the manor. But she didn't believe Lady Fiona would refuse Aggie the time off.

Chloe waited until Isabel awoke, to be sure she was well enough, before she made her way back to the manor, exhausted from the excitement of the day.

She climbed into the carriage, thinking today was the happiest day of her life. She'd very likely saved a young girl's life, Hawk breathed new life into this dying town and Chloe was falling in love with Ian.

She closed her eyes, resting her weary head back upon the seat, wanting nothing more in that instant than to be able to fall into Ian's arms.

CURSING himself for not adjusting the books sooner, Edward snarled. It was only that Fiona had never taken much of an interest in the household accounts. He couldn't allow her to uncover the truth now. And if she did, he couldn't let her share the knowledge with his royal highness.

His brain hurt as he stared at the missing ledgers he'd hidden in his room. He could blackmail Lady Fiona, perhaps. He could threaten to tell Ian that she could walk and that there was nothing wrong with her legs. But was that enough to prevent her from taking action against him?

Somehow he didn't think so.

He could threaten to tell Ian the truth about his father... but if he did that, his royal highness would castrate him and hang his balls from his ears.

That wouldn't do, either. What good would money do him if he weren't alive to enjoy it?

He cursed the constable for being such a bumbling fool. He'd given the man ample clues as to Hawk's identity. He'd even learned about Miss Simon's intended rendezvous with him from Emily, the bigmouthed prostitute at the Pale Ale. He'd given that information to the constable, but to no fruition. The bloody fool had, instead of catching a thief, stumbled upon two lovers rolling about the fields like rabbits in heat. The thought was disgusting—that Ian could lower himself to such depths was deplorable. Miss Simon was no more than a filthy commoner, with no proper morals. What sort of girl went about pretending to be a physician and ogling men's and women's naked forms? It was absolutely despicable.

He would have come straight out and told the constable who Hawk was, but he knew he would have suffered consequences if he had. It could never be Edward who betrayed Julian's second son.

Edward's mother had been a servant, perhaps, but he shared the same father as Julian. He was quite certain the only reason Julian sent him away with Fiona was because Julian hadn't wished to suffer his presence. How ironic it was that the son Julian would place upon the throne was little better than Edward—a bastard child.

It grated on his nerves.

As for Ian, the bugger, it did Edward much good to see him squirm, to have him come to Edward for his paltry allowances, only so Edward could refuse him.

Vengeance could be so sweet.

Fiona never once guessed at his connection to Julian. Despite that they shared much of the same look, it had never even occurred to her to question Edward's birth. She had always assumed and treated him as though he were no better than her own servants, ordering him about, taking him to task—Edward this, Edward that!

She was nothing but a silly twit. For twenty-eight years she'd pined for a man who'd obviously never loved her.

In the beginning Edward hadn't felt this way about her. In fact, he'd felt somewhat of a kinship with Fiona, because they'd both been cast away like so much rubbish. But Fiona had looked beyond him so many years that Edward felt nothing for her now but resentment. He felt it was his right to have this money after all his years of servitude. He'd been loyal to her to no avail. That had gotten him precisely nowhere.

He sighed. What to do... what to do...

He stared at the books, willing the answers to come to light.

Light.

He could burn them...

But if he did, Fiona would continue to question their whereabouts. Only what if he burned them, along with the others... and perhaps the entire house?

He considered that avenue. The rest of the books were in Lady Fiona's room... if he burned one, he would need to burn them all.

He could make it look like an accident….

TODAY WAS THE DAY.

The charade must come to an end.

Merrick intended to take full responsibility for the necklace he'd stolen. The jeweler in Edinburgh who'd purchased it had agreed to hold it until Merrick returned, on the promise that Merrick would pay him double the money he'd been given for it. But there was no guarantee that he could safely return it to his mother now that it was out of his hands, and she must know what actions he had taken.

After leaving Chloe, he'd gone straight to his bedroom, intending to clean up before facing his mother. Gad, but he'd loved to have bathed Chloe, too… massage those lovely shoulders and ease the aches he knew she would feel in the aftermath of their loving.

The entire world had a new perspective this morn. Everything was clear to him.

The constable would be taken care of once Merrick was able to fully address the matter. But, at any rate, Ian hadn't any more reason to don his mask and once Hawk joined the ranks of Glen Abbey's legends, the constable would have no more need to make Hawk's capture his life's mission. Merrick would see to it that his brother had whatever he needed. He would make certain his father released Glen Abbey Manor and see to it that it was restored to its former glory. For all the injustices suffered here—never mind those committed against himself—he intended to make reparations. God's truth, if his father wasn't man enough to do it, Merrick would do it for him.

As for Edward, well, the steward wouldn't be a problem, either, because Merrick fully intended to rake that bugger over hot coals, then deposit his charcoaled arse on the street. He never trusted that shifty-eyed fool.

Finally, as for Merrick's father, he didn't have the first inkling how he would react to the news of his bride, but Merrick didn't give a bloody damn at this point. If he must forfeit his crown, his position, everything he had come to know, he would willingly do so for Chloe.

Alas, his mother was another matter entirely.

He couldn't begin to anticipate how that reunion might go. Some part of him felt certain she would embrace him, but some part of him feared she would not. At twenty-eight, how did one stand before one's own mother for the very first time?

What did one say?

What did one do?

Whatever the outcome, Merrick intended to procure for her the finest care—nothing against Chloe, but he selfishly wanted his wife by his side. However, before he revealed himself to Fiona, there was one last thing he knew he must do. For the sake of everyone involved, it was past time to put Hawk to rest once and for all.

In broad daylight Merrick summoned his motley band together and told them the truth. He trusted them to keep what he would tell them close to their vests. He had to trust them, because he needed their help to put an end to Hawk once and for all. After today, Hawk would live and breathe no more.

With open mouths, they sat in the middle of a field on Glen Abbey's parklands—at Merrick's request, unmasked. Their expressions revealed only stunned surprise over Merrick's confession. None of them had— nor could they have—suspected, for he and Ian were identical twins.

Despite himself, Merrick had come to care for these men as though they were his own fellows; he wanted them to take no more risks with their lives or with the welfare of their families.

"What of our children? How will we feed them? How will we support them?" the men questioned irately.

"Every one of you has more than enough coin to invest in your newly acquired land. I suggest you put it to good use."

Rusty's gaze snapped up to meet Merrick's in surprise. He was the only one who'd caught Merrick's choice of words. "Our land?"

Merrick nodded. "Yours."

Angus asked, "So you're going to give it to us? But I thought Ian said it wasn't his to give."

"It wasn't, but I'm certain it's mine—for now—and I am giving it to you. In any case, I cannot believe my brother would begrudge you this small gift for your loyalty."

"Och," Donald said in surprise.

"Go home," Merrick charged them. He mounted his horse, eager to return to Chloe. "Go and burn your masks," he instructed them, then grinned. "And while you're at it, buy a boar or two. I want to smell a bonfire on the horizon tonight. It's time to celebrate!"

"That's it?" asked Rusty, his face crestfallen, looking suddenly melancholic as Merrick prepared to leave. "Not you... nor Hawk... I mean, you won't be..."

Merrick instinctively understood what Rusty was asking and he meant to put the man's mind at ease. He looked pointedly at Rusty Broun, though he was speaking to each and every one of them. He had learned so much from them and their friendship humbled him. "My door—and I'm certain I speak for my brother, as well—will always remain open to you gentlemen."

"Did you hear that?" Donald exclaimed in a whisper, ribbing Angus. "He called us gentlemen!"

"Aye, an' 'e gave us land," said Angus.

Overhearing their banter, Merrick grinned, pleased with their enthusiasm. "Under one condition," he reminded them. "If you want that land, you have this final task to accomplish all together... make certain Hawk never robs again. Put him to death once and for all," he commanded, "and the land is yours to do with as you will." He whirled his mount to ride away, but peered over his shoulder. "Oh, and when you're through," he shouted over his shoulder as he rode away, "you're all invited to attend a wedding!"

CHAPTER 20

"*T*here you are, madame," said Edward. "The remainder of the books... as you requested."

"Oh, good!" Fiona exclaimed. "You found them!" She had begun to wonder if he would ever deliver them, but felt far more at ease now that he had. If Edward had something to hide, she reasoned, he wouldn't have brought them to her with such a cheery demeanor. "Where were they?"

"Hidden under too many layers of dust," Edward disclosed. "But here they are at last."

Fiona sighed, relieved. "Thank you, Edward. Will you bring me my tea?" she requested. "Would you mind terribly?"

"Not at all, madame," Edward said, turning at once to do her bidding, gritting his teeth over the injustices of having to fetch tea for his half-brother's cast-off mistress.

He was born for better things than this.

But, as a last gesture of humility, he personally made her tea, then delivered it to her. He set the cup down on the night table, but she scarcely noticed it, she was so engrossed in the blasted ledgers.

He closed the door, cursing her along with Julian's

bastard sons. "Happy reading," he said beneath his breath.

CHLOE KNOCKED SOFTLY on Fiona's door. She was growing quite concerned as Fiona hadn't called for Chloe's attendance in days. It was very unlike her.

"Who is it?"

"Chloe."

"Come in," Fiona bade her, but there was something odd in her tone.

Chloe opened the door and was startled to find such a disarray within the room. Walking past row upon row of ledgers, Chloe eyed them curiously. "Good Lord, my lady, what's all this about?"

"Please... close the door," Fiona said in a hush. The expression on her face was that of consternation.

Chloe carefully retreated through the precarious stacks to close the door, then made her way back through the mountains of books to Lady Fiona's bedside.

"Look," Fiona said, urging her closer. She motioned for Chloe to sit on the bed. Chloe did as she was asked, noticing that Fiona's fingers trembled as she opened a particular book and set it before Chloe.

Chloe hadn't the first inkling what it was she was looking at.

"Let me explain," Fiona said, her voice trembly. It was clear to Chloe that she was quite distraught. "These are the household ledgers. They go back to the day when I took over Glen Abbey Manor... er, rather, the day Ian's father took it over."

Chloe drew her brows together in confusion. "I don't understand. I thought Ian's father was a merchant."

Fiona shook her head, her eyes full of regret. "God forgive me for all the lies. I was so ashamed. Ian's father was not a merchant, Chloe," Fiona said, her eyes misting. "He was...well... he was, as I have said, a prince."

For an instant Chloe thought Fiona might have gone completely mad, but something about the desperate look in her blue eyes convinced her. She remembered the tales and said, blinking, "So it's true? You married a prince?"

Fiona shook her head again, and this time her expression was melancholy as she told Chloe about Ian's real father.

"I'm afraid there is so much more," she added, but Chloe didn't know what to say.

Fiona's eyes glazed over with tears and her expression turned to one of such terrible sorrow that Chloe wanted only to hug her—and she might have, but one did not hug Lady Fiona. She was sweet and kind, for certain, but there was a distance she kept from everyone, including her son.

Her eyes met Chloe's and they were full of torment. "Ian has a brother," Fiona said, nodding, tears pooling in her eyes. "His name is Merrick."

Chloe's hand lifted to her mouth in shock.

"A twin," Fiona revealed.

Something snapped in Chloe's head; clarity came to her at once.

"Oh!" Chloe said, holding her hand up for Lady Fiona to pause in her storytelling, "Just a moment." She hurried back to her room to grab the ring from where she had hidden it beneath her pillow, and then she returned, proffering the ring for Lady Fiona's inspection. "Do you know what this is?" she asked.

The look of shock on Fiona's face was palpable. Her cheeks paled and her eyes grew wide. She seized the ring from Chloe. "Where did you get this?" she asked frantically.

Chloe knew suddenly just as surely as she stood in front of Lady Fiona that it wasn't Ian she loved. "Your son gave it to me," she said.

"That's impossible!" Fiona declared with certainty. "Ian hasn't the first inkling of his past or he would have confronted me ages ago. Do you know what this is?" she asked Chloe, holding up the ring.

Chloe shook her head.

"It is the royal crest of Meridian."

Chloe stared at the ruby stone.

She had known something was different about him. But if Ian was Merrick, where was Ian?

Chloe sat, stunned, staring at the ring.

Fiona began to weep. "Dearest God... it must be Merrick!" She clutched the ring to her breast as a heart-wrenching sob tore from her throat. To Chloe, it sounded as though it had come from the very depths of her soul. "I didn't even know him." She peered up at Chloe. "Where is he now?" Tears streamed from her eyes.

Chloe shrugged, at a loss for words. He had come to her last night, but she daren't confess as much to Fiona. The mere thought of it burned her cheeks.

"You must find him, Chloe," Fiona charged her. "It is imperative! Let me show you something."

Again, she returned to the ledger. "We are supposed to keep a detailed accounting of every penny we spend at Glen Abbey Manor. If ever we spent too much, Julian —Merrick's father—has threatened to remove us from the estate. But look at this..." She pointed to one, two, three entries that had no detailed explanation for the sums withdrawn. Each line of withdrawal held an extraordinary sum.

"What does that mean?" Chloe asked her.

Fiona shook her head. "That's just it. I have no idea! Edward claims they are miscellaneous expenditures and claims, furthermore, that they are monies he dispatched to Ian."

She lifted her cold cup of tea from the night table and guzzled from it, her hands trembling. "I don't believe it! Knowing what I know of my son, he would not take money and hoard it. And he would not lie to me." She set the teacup down, and made a face as it rattled over the saucer. "Absolutely disgusting! But I'm so thirsty!"

"Shall I go get you something to drink?" Chloe asked, wanting to help but not knowing what to do.

"No!" Fiona said firmly. "Do not concern yourself with me. You must go and find my son."

"Yes, madame," Chloe said.

"Please, Chloe, do not call me madame!" Fiona reprimanded. "Go, now! And please hurry!"

Hearing the hysteria in Fiona's voice, Chloe wasted little time. She went, at once, to search for Merrick.

EDWARD HAD BEEN WAITING in the shadows for his opportunity to sneak into Lady Fiona's room, but Chloe came knocking and he'd stood there in the hall for what seemed an eternity while those two spoke in hushed tones inside the bedroom.

At one point, he'd put his ear to the door only to hear what he could hear, but their conversation had been reduced to muffled whispers.

This was not good.

At last, Chloe emerged. With a wary glance down each end of the hall, she rushed toward the stairwell.

Edward followed.

The way she was behaving, he feared she must

know something. Fiona must have spilled her guts to the girl.

He couldn't take any chances.

He followed her all the way to the stables, lifted up a board that had fallen and waited. When her back was to him, he rushed forward, smacking her once on the back of the head. She crumpled without a sound, like a paper flower doused with water.

CHAPTER 21

*M*errick had but one thing left to do before confronting his mother.

He spent the greater part of the evening at the cottage penning a letter to his father. He'd needed complete peace to consider how to best address the matter. It was a delicate situation; he was going to marry Chloe and he didn't intend to wait to do it. If his father wished it, he would remarry her in a traditional ceremony in Meridian, but that would be left to his father to decide. For all Merrick knew, if he could deny one son, he could surely deny another. He might well disown Merrick for what he was about to do, but that was a chance Merrick was willing to take. If he must live on the streets in order to be with Chloe, he would gladly do so only to be by her side. He finished the letter and went into town to hire a messenger to carry the letter to the London apartment where he and his father had taken up temporary residence, then made his way back to the manor. The distant smoke of a bonfire caught his scent and he smiled, pleased that his men had taken his advice. In fact, he felt damned good about the decisions he'd made.

But, as he neared Glen Abbey Manor, he spied the orange glow in the evening sky and frowned. It was far too bright to be only a bonfire, he realized, and the smoky scent filling the air grew thicker as he drew nearer.

His heart racing at the obvious conclusion, He spurred his mount into a gallop.

Glen Abbey Manor was on fire!

A bellow tore from his lips as he reined in before the raging inferno.

His first thought was for Chloe; his second for his mother. But Merrick knew his mother was unable to fend for herself and it was Fiona he knew he must go after first.

Bracing himself for the worst, he kicked open the front door. Smoke was heavy, but there were no visible flames. Fortunately, Fiona's bedroom was on the ground floor and he made his way there first.

It was in the gallery he met the wall of flames, angry tongues of fire licking the walls, searing through portraits, reducing them to shriveled caricatures before devouring them whole.

Just beyond the gallery, he could spy the door to his mother's room. Merrick stood in the hall, trying to determine how best to reach her when his mother's door suddenly flew open.

For the briefest instant she stood there on both feet, choking on the smoke, and then an explosion of flames roared past her, knocking her backward.

He didn't stop to think what it meant that she had been standing. He sucked in a breath as he leapt through the flames toward her. He reached her by the sheer will of God and lifted her into his arms, ignoring the slivers of flames that tore through his shirt and torched his skin.

Choking back the smoke from his own lungs, he made his way toward the window, knowing there would be precious little time to waste once he broke the glass. With his mother en tow, he slammed his fist against the window, shattering glass. Not caring that it cut his flesh, he continued to whack at the shards until there were none remaining to bar the way. Then, he slipped through the window with his mother on his back. They made it out barely in time. The fire exploded into the room, engulfing it fully.

Spewing smoke from his lungs, Merrick dragged his mother out far enough that she would be safe from the flames.

By now the servants had begun to filter out of the house. One of the maids came scurrying to Fiona's side to aid her mistress, holding out her arms so that Fiona might lay in her lap and her head would not rest on the dirty ground. Merrick deposited her into the woman's arms. The maid wept softly over Fiona's still form.

Peering up at the house on fire, Merrick's heart wrenched painfully. The servants' quarters were on the third floor, he realized. Chloe's room was on the third floor.

He scanned the faces on the lawn, noting at once that Chloe wasn't among them. Panic seized him, taking his breath away. "Where is Chloe?" he asked.

The servants all shrugged, each in turn as he met their frightened gazes.

"Oh, dear God—no!" he shouted, and he ran toward the house. But the front door was barred by a solid wall of flame. The house was completely engulfed.

He had no inkling how many came to restrain him, but he fought desperately to get into the house aflame. They wouldn't release him. Speaking to him in words he could not comprehend because his heart was screaming, they dragged him away from the inferno as the roof caved in right before his eyes.

No! It was too late!

He sank to his knees. "Chloe," he cried, swallowing the knot that rose like a mountain in his throat. He suddenly couldn't breathe. He knelt on the lawn, numb as grief swept through him like a dark plague.

They dragged him backward to where his mother lay.

Fiona began to cough and spew, waking. She looked up into his face, tears filling her eyes. Her hand fell open, revealing his ring, but Merrick was too stupefied to acknowledge it.

His heart felt as though it had been ripped from his chest.

"Merrick," she said softly, calling him by name.

Her arms stretched toward him and he couldn't help himself. Like a broken child, he fell into his mother's arms, weeping, not caring who would see.

CHLOE MOANED IN PAIN. "You'll never get away with this."

"Of course I will," Edward replied, his mood entirely unruffled by her threat.

Chloe's head hurt. She felt as though he had surely cracked her skull. "Fiona already knows you were embezzling. She'll tell Ian. He'll come looking for you."

The horrid man had her trussed up and twisted down on the carriage floor while he sat above her, casually placing a foot on her ribs as though she were some sort of hunting conquest.

He laughed a laugh that grated upon her nerves. "Fiona is dead," he said with certainty, "Ian is worthless."

Dread swept through her. "What have you done to her?"

He peered down at Chloe and smirked, digging his heel deeper into her ribs. She winced, but refused to cry out. She didn't intend to give him the satisfaction.

"She had a little accident with her lamp," he disclosed, his tone smug. "It seems to have turned over during the night and caught the draperies afire. You know how these things happen. Tsk, tsk. Haven't you told her more than once she must not leave the lamp lit?"

Chloe's heart cried out for poor Fiona stuck in her bed. She imagined what it must feel like to be trapped by the failings of your own body. Anger surged through her. Chloe wanted Edward to be afraid. God help her, she wanted to strangle him with her own bare hands!

"If you have no fear of Ian," she told him, clenching her teeth, "perhaps you may of Merrick."

He peered down at her, cocking his head, his brows colliding. "How is it you know that name?"

Despite that Chloe was afraid, anger was her ally. The tiny note of panic in his voice gave her strength. She smirked at him. "He'll hunt you down. And he'll kill you with his own bare hands. Make no mistake." That was… if Merrick had the first inkling where to look for her… or even to look for her at all.

Chloe eyed Edward with disgust, seeing clearly for the first time in so long. She had mistakenly blamed Ian for the trials brought upon their kinsmen, but in truth it was Edward who held Glen Abbey's purse strings, raising rents and bleeding them dry. It was always Edward who came to collect monies. It was Edward who'd come to baldly inform her that the cottage was no longer her own and that she must vacate the premises at once. It was Edward's greed that killed poor Ana, she realized, and it was his wickedness that was slowly ravaging Glen Abbey.

She must somehow get herself free and find Merrick, she thought desperately. It might be too late for Fiona, but it wasn't for the others.

Edward, the fiend, must pay for his sins.

CHAPTER 22

*T*he manor was in ruins.

Grief stricken, Merrick retreated with Fiona to the cottage.

Everything was destroyed, from the portraits in the gallery to the ledgers that were left in Fiona's room. Merrick had assured her that he'd had no knowledge of the fact that his father had ordered them kept. It should have been a first clue that every last ledger could be found on the estate. Merrick, who had kept the books in Meridian, had never once had one forwarded for his inspection. In fact, he'd never even heard of Glen Abbey until he'd read his father's letters.

Merrick would have told Fiona about the letters, but he'd determined that Ryo was right. It was his father's place to tell Fiona, not his.

Thank God they'd found no trace of Chloe within the house. All the servants made it out unharmed. His heart had never felt emptier than it had in that instant when he'd thought he'd lost her. And he still might lose her, but not if he had anything to do with it. His mother claimed that after Chloe showed her the ring, she'd sent Chloe to search for him.

That was the last Fiona had seen of her.

Clearly, Chloe hadn't found Merrick, but it appeared someone else had found Chloe.

Edward was missing.

The constable came to make his report, but of course. And, in speaking with Tolly, Merrick determined that he was, indeed, a good man, who wanted nothing more than to save his beloved town from ruin. Merrick was honest with him and told him the truth—or most of it—that he wasn't Ian. Tolly had likely guessed the rest of the tale, but it was understood that the matter would be dropped. It was no longer to be a concern. He'd already heard the news; Hawk was dead. As for locating Edward, Merrick awaited his men. One last time they would ride together, but this time with deadly purpose. The carriage was missing; Edward wouldn't get far. And when he caught the fool, Merrick intended to be the man's judge and his jury.

EDWARD STOPPED at an inn for the night, leaving Chloe to freeze to death in the carriage. Her toes were numb from the cold and her fingers tingling from lack of circulation.

She hadn't the first inkling where Edward was taking her, but she sensed that now was her chance to escape. Whatever he intended to do with her, she knew it couldn't be good. If he were willing to dispose of a woman he'd worked for for twenty-eight years, Chloe knew he had no reason to spare her. It was not very ladylike, but she cursed him beneath her breath. Not only was she trussed like an animal, but he'd tied her to the carriage as well, and she was bound so well that she could barely breathe, much less move.

Shivering against the cold night air, she was unable

to scream for the yards of material he'd shoved in her mouth. Her jaws were beginning to hurt.

She heard voices outside and tried to scream for help, but her bellows sounded more like strangled murmurs. Desperate to free herself, she squirmed until her arms were chafed and her body ached, attempting in vain to kick at the carriage.

She feared she would never be free. But suddenly the carriage door opened, and Merrick's beautiful face appeared before her like a dark, blue-eyed guardian angel. All that was missing was his wings.

Tears sprung to her eyes at once.

"Chloe," he said, sounding relieved as he pulled her at once from the carriage and removed the gag from her mouth.

Unmasked, his men stood at his back. For the first time Chloe saw their faces. They were all-too familiar to her and she had to laugh.

Donald Lowson, whose wife had only just borne him a babe. Angus Macpherson, whose brother owned the Pale Ale. Rusty she had already guessed. Lonny Macpherson, Angus's youngest brother. And Jamie Brewer, Emily's sweet, skinny cousin.

"Miss Chloe," Jamie said, nodding. "Emily says ta tell ye that she's sorry. She said you'd know what that means."

Chloe smiled gently as Merrick worked quickly to untie her bindings. When she was free at last, she cried out in relief and threw herself into Merrick's arms. His expression was sober, but when his gaze met hers, she saw the love there and felt safe at last.

"Where is Edward?"

"Gone," Merrick told her. "He untied one of the horses from the carriage and fled.

"Come," Merrick said, taking Chloe by the hand. Leaving his men to fend for themselves, he led Chloe into the inn, certain she was tired. It wasn't as though there was a house left to return to, anyway. Fiona was sleeping peacefully at the cottage; Chloe needed her rest, as well. Tomorrow was soon enough to face the rest of their lives.

THANKING GOD he'd reached Chloe in time, Merrick procured a room, ordered a bath, and lifted Chloe into his arms to carry her to their room.

He didn't want to live without her.

Chloe clung to him, not speaking, clearly in shock. He brought her inside and closed the door. She gently touched his forehead. "You've burnt yourself."

"It's nothing," he swore.

"Did he hurt you?" Merrick demanded. He would strangle the bastard when he found him.

She shook her head and started to weep. "I'm so sorry about your mother," she said, burying her face into her hands. "I should never have left her."

Merrick smiled at her, pulling her hands away so she could see his face. Tenderly he brushed his fingers through her hair. "My mother is fine," he reassured. "More so than you realize, in fact."

Chloe furrowed her brow, tears swelling in her eyes. "What do you mean?"

"I mean, she can walk," Merrick said simply, shaking his head in wonderment that she'd kept it a secret for so long. "It seems it was all a ploy."

Chloe narrowed her eyes. "So it's true. But why?"

"To get you to come to the manor."

"I don't understand."

Merrick grinned. "She was attempting to play matchmaker, I'm afraid—and it worked, but not quite as she expected."

Chloe merely looked at him, studying him. It was

quite clear she wanted to say something but didn't know how to ask.

There was a knock upon the door. Merrick left her long enough to open it and to help the attendants set up her bath. Once they were gone, he returned to the bed and, ignoring her protest, undressed her.

CHLOE'S HEART squeezed her painfully.

She felt a sudden overwhelming shyness, studying his face, trying to see the differences between the brothers. Without Ian present to compare them, it was utterly impossible. They had the same face, the same body, even, it seemed, the same voice.

Everything she'd known about this man was a lie— from the very first to the very last. And yet... she was glad.

Merrick lifted her from the bed and put her in the bath, then started to massage her shoulders. Chloe knew she was stiff beneath his touch, but she couldn't help it. This wasn't Ian. Nor was he Hawk. And she knew absolutely nothing of Merrick.

Except that he had loved her so sweetly.

The memory of that night brought a blush to her body that had absolutely nothing to do with the heat of the bath.

"Does that feel good?" he asked, his voice gentle.

Chloe nodded, feeling awkward.

She waited a moment, letting the steam calm her, and then she confessed, "I showed your mother the ring."

"I know," he said. His tone was sober. "It's all true, Chloe."

Chloe inhaled sharply.

Her hopes dashed. She hadn't any chance when he was Ian. She hadn't been good enough for a simple lord. Merrick was a prince—someday to be a king. She hadn't anything at all to offer him—no dowry at all.

Not a thing.

Once upon a time, Fiona had made the mistake of aiming too high and look where it had gotten her.

Alone.

Merrick moved around the bathtub, washing her legs beneath the water, massaging them gently, lifting up her ankles to inspect the rope burns—not at all duties suited to a man of his stature. In fact, he was behaving more like a servant, in truth.

"Chloe," he began, and his tone was far too sober. Her heart began to pound against her ribs. She held her breath, knowing what was to come. He would tell her she was sweet and that he'd enjoyed himself thoroughly and he would explain how unsuited they were.

He would apologize and then he would leave her. Men like Merrick did not linger over their mistakes, nor would he suffer for it like Chloe would.

Already, her reputation had suffered.

Still, she couldn't quite think of him as a mistake.

She averted her gaze, fighting back tears.

She could go on with her own plans for her life... find a way to practice her medicine. There was so much good she could do with her life.

HE TOOK her gently by the hand, and for the longest moment Merrick couldn't speak, so full was his heart, so thick was his throat with emotion.

As he looked at her lying within the tub, so vulnerable, he knew he wanted to take care of her for the rest of his life. This is what he was born for—not thrones or crowns.

In truth, he'd never been satisfied with the power of

his position. It never made him smile, nor had it filled his heart as Chloe did.

And suddenly everything was clearer than it had been in ages. He didn't want to rule a nation; he wanted Ian to have the chance.

He knew, with a certainty he had never experienced before this moment, that he didn't wish to be king. For twenty-eight years, he'd had everything his heart desired, and nothing ever pleased him. In the few weeks he'd been here, he'd learned more about himself through Chloe's eyes and through the hearts of the men his brother called friends. These men weren't kings or dukes or earls or barons, but he knew this for certain... they would, indeed, kill to protect those they loved, and he needn't pay them a fortune to do it. They looked after their own, and they loved Chloe as a sister. As soon as they'd been told what had happened, every single man had gone after his gun and his horse. He hadn't had to ask them to join him.

Merrick had never had friends before now.

He'd rarely smiled.

Never loved.

Until now.

"Do you think..." His voice broke. "That you could be happy to be a simple farmer's wife?"

CHLOE'S EYES BURNED. Was he trying to marry her off to some unfortunate man? God help her, she shook her head, not comprehending. Surely he didn't mean that he would give up everything only to be with her?

"I want you to be my wife," he said with sincerity and conviction. "I want wee ones like Rusty Broun's who'll climb on my back and beg for rides. I want to be smothered in kisses by sweet-faced daughters. I want to teach my sons to hunt."

He made it sound like heaven on earth, but she knew he couldn't possibly want that—not when he could have any woman he desired and any life he chose. Her eyes filled with tears. "How could I ever ask you to give up so much only to be with me?"

Merrick's eyes, as she peered into them, moistened with tears, mirroring her own. "Chloe... when I thought I'd lost you tonight, I realized... my life is nothing without you. Nothing, do you understand? I am not Ian," he said. "Forgive me for that. But I am the same man who has loved you from the instant I saw you."

Chloe swallowed, terrified to believe in him, terrified to hope, terrified to lose him. "But... you were born to be a king," she argued.

He shook his head. "No, Chloe. I was born to be your husband. It will be my life's joy to care for you until the day I die—hopefully in your arms."

Chloe's eyes overflowed with tears. "You mean it truly?" she asked, overcome with joy.

He nodded without hesitation. "I will build you a hospital here where you can treat patients for free. We can stay in Glen Abbey, raise our children together—let Ian take my place, if he will. He doesn't realize it yet, but it's his crown to do with as he pleases. He is the crusader... not me. I can see him now... helping the people of our nation."

Chloe's throat convulsed. Her lips trembled. Her heart felt as though it would burst. She shook her head, wanting to believe in happily-ever-afters, but sorely afraid to. "You would loathe me someday for making you give up so much."

Merrick, too, shook his head very adamantly. "No, my love. I was imprisoned by my life before. Now I am free."

"Truly?" she asked.

222

He nodded. "Truly."

"Then, yes," she said, nodding happily. "Yes!"

Merrick reached out and took her into his arms, not caring that she would wet his clothing. "Marry me tomorrow," he demanded, spinning her about, and Chloe laughed.

She wrapped her arms about his neck and kissed him joyfully. And then, she suddenly felt extraordinarily wicked with him holding her naked to his chest. She smiled at him.

Recognizing that look in her eyes Merrick grinned, and they fell together upon the bed. Chloe untied his cravat, her gaze never leaving his. Smiling impishly, she tossed it to the floor.

Merrick shivered at her look, at the slow, deliberate way she removed his clothing. "I have corrupted you, I fear," he said, but he grinned anyway, and his body hardened with her touch.

Chloe nodded, her eyes shining with tears.

Lying gloriously naked before him, her skin pink from the warm water, her lips wet from his kisses and her hair flowing down her back, she looked like a temptress... a siren.

When he was naked, as well, she rose from the bed, luring him into the tub. They stood facing each other a moment and then she pushed him down into the water and sat on his lap in the most scandalous fashion. Her body fit over his like a velvety glove.

Indeed, she was made for him, her body tight and warm and soft.

"I will give you all the children you desire," she whispered.

"And I will love you until I die," he promised, his voice hoarse with desire.

And he meant it. With every fiber of his being.

Chloe began to undulate over him. It was a wicked

dance they performed, writhing in the tub together. She rode until he could bear it no longer and then he stood, holding her close so that they wouldn't separate, walking with her to the bed, laying her down.

Chloe moaned softly, writhing beneath him as he covered her completely. Pushing himself inside her, he increased the tempo, burying himself deeper and deeper with every thrust, until it seemed they truly were one. When at last they came together, the two of them collapsed wearily into each other's arms and fell asleep till the morning light.

*M*errick sat at his desk in the little cottage, penning the final draft of his letter to his brother. It was long and involved, with explanations that were better left for a face-to-face discussion. He blew a sigh, wadding up the paper, tossing it in the bin with all the rest.

"Dammit all," he said, frustrated by his lack of verbosity.

"What is it, darling?" Chloe asked, coming up behind him to massage his shoulders.

They married a month before in a small, but lovely ceremony that was attended by the entire town. Isabel, Aggie's little sister, carried posies, smiling as she'd tossed them at every pew along the aisle. Aggie both sewed and carried Chloe's train. Evidently, she was a master seamstress.

For her part, Fiona sat, all the while weeping, in the front pew, with Constable Tolly patting her hand.

Rusty, along with his wife and three daughters, all prettily dressed in new outfits from Mr. Duncan's newly restocked general store, sat behind Fiona.

Donald Lowson, his wife and two-month-old

daughter sat in the back row—lest she begin to wail again. Merrick hadn't minded. He wanted a few of his own someday.

"I simply do not know what to say," he confessed. Ian had yet to learn the truth and Merrick couldn't find the words to explain all that had transpired, all that he felt. He wanted to know his brother—but more than that, he wanted to somehow make amends for all the years Ian must have felt like a beggar in his own home.

Chloe rubbed gently at his neck, calming his nerves. His lovely wife had a way of making everything perfectly clear. "Are you still certain you wish to give it all up?"

Merrick pulled out a clean parchment. "Yes," he said, "Without question." He stared at the paper a moment and then realized he needn't say much at all—at least until they were face-to-face. Until then, Ryo would explain the rest. All Merrick needed to do was to give up the ring. So, he penned the following.

My dearest brother, wear it in good health.

And with the letter completed, he removed the ring from his finger, wrapped it in a kerchief and waited for Rusty to arrive. He trusted Rusty to deliver it safely to its destination.

"There. It is done," he said, and he sighed in relief. "No more worries."

They were in somewhat cramped quarters until the new house was complete. Every last man in Glen Abbey had come together to rebuild the manor. Merrick, along with the rest of the men, had rolled up his sleeves to help reconstruct his mother's home. He labored with his hands day by day, building calluses along with his home, but he came to bed every night feeling blissfully tired and complete—satisfied in a way he had never known.

There was little that survived the fire. A few baubles here and there. Most everything else was gone—save for the aviary, the stables and his mother's rose garden.

He turned in his chair to face his wife, reveling in the beauty of her smile. "Do you realize we're alone until Mother returns?" Fiona had ventured out for a picnic and a walk with Constable Tolly. He raised a brow meaningfully.

Chloe giggled.

She tapped him gently on the bridge of his nose. "I suppose you wish to try again for that daughter you so desire?" She sighed, as though it were the greatest of burdens, but it was betrayed by her impish grin.

Merrick shrugged. "Or son. It matters not to me."

She bent to kiss him sweetly, wrapping her arms about his neck so possessively that it made him shudder with desire. His loins stirred at once. She never failed to do this to him, rouse him to incredible heights of passion.

"What say we retire to the bedroom?" he suggested.

"Yes, of course, Your Majesty," she teased, whispering in his ear, "Anything you say, Your Majesty."

Merrick grunted as he lifted her up and carried her into the bedroom. She said, "You will always be my king."

"And you my queen."

Surely, as much as they had coupled in the last month, she should be increasing by now... but oh, well... Merrick was having the time of his life trying.

"About that daughter," he said as he lay her down on the bed, grinning mischievously.

"Son," she returned with a smile and lifted her chin.

"Whichever," he said. And then, "I love you, flower."

"I love you, too," Chloe whispered back.

And they made love, whispering sweet words to each other, promising to adore each other for the rest of their days.

THE STORY ISN'T OVER - NOT QUITE!

Chloe and Merrick may have found happy ever after, but the story isn't over. I hope you'll follow Ian to London to see what mischief he discovers—most notably, a fiery lady by the name of Claire Wentworth. A Crown for a Lady is coming October 22, 2019

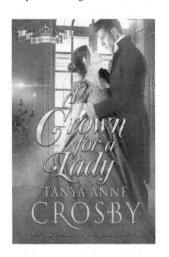

A HEARTFELT THANK YOU!

Thank you from the bottom of my heart for reading Seduced by a Prince! There are millions of titles out there, and I'm honored you decided to read one of mine.

If you enjoyed this book, please consider posting a review. Reviews help other readers discover our books and I sincerely appreciate every single one, no matter how long or short.

Would you like to know when my next book is available? Sign up for my newsletter and follow me on social media:

Facebook: facebook.com/tanyaannecrosby
Twitter at @tanyaannecrosby
Instagram at tanyaannecrosby

Also, please follow me on BookBub to be notified of deals and new releases.

Let's hang out! I have a Facebook group:

Tanya's Book Tribe

I'm also a member of the Jewels of Historical Romance. I hope you'll visit our Facebook group, the Jewels Salon. Read on for links to our Fabulous Firsts collections, two six book anthologies featuring starters for our most beloved series—each set is just 99c!

Thank you again for reading and for your support.

Taraya Anne Crosby

Once Upon a Kiss
Angel of Fire
Viking's Prize

REDEEMABLE ROGUES
Happily Ever After
Perfect In My Sight
McKenzie's Bride
Kissed by a Rogue
Thirty Ways to Leave a Duke
A Perfectly Scandalous Proposal

ANTHOLOGIES & NOVELLAS
Lady's Man
Married at Midnight
The Winter Stone

ROMANTIC SUSPENSE
Speak No Evil
Tell No Lies
Leave No Trace

MAINSTREAM FICTION
The Girl Who Stayed
The Things We Leave Behind
Redemption Song
Reprisal
Everyday Lies

ABOUT THE AUTHOR

Tanya Anne Crosby is the New York Times and USA Today bestselling author of thirty novels. She has been featured in magazines, such as People, Romantic Times and Publisher's Weekly, and her books have been translated into eight languages. Her first novel was published in 1992 by Avon Books, where Tanya was hailed as "one of Avon's fastest rising stars." Her fourth book was chosen to launch the company's Avon Romantic Treasure imprint.

Known for stories charged with emotion and humor and filled with flawed characters Tanya is an award-winning author, journalist, and editor, and her novels have garnered reader praise and glowing critical reviews. She and her writer husband split their time between Charleston, SC, where she was raised, and northern Michigan, where the couple make their home.

For more information
Website
Email
Newsletter

Lightning Source UK Ltd.
Milton Keynes UK
UKHW020744150822
407319UK00012B/2629